"You're beautiful, and you know it."

Dominic laughed. "That might be true, but I don't mind hearing it from you. Compliments are unimportant... unless they're from someone you respect."

"You don't respect me," Meredith insisted.

"I respect the hell out of you. Why do you think I've kept my hands to myself all these years? Sex is easy. There's nothing about you that's easy. Everything about you is complicated."

Meredith was desperately trying to hang on to reality. To keep from getting wrapped up in Dominic.

But if he kept saying things like that...

"Well, let's uncomplicate things, then. I'm fully aware of your mantra, Nic. And I'm happy to live by your rules."

"And what do you think those are?"

"Like you said, sex is easy. We clearly both want each other. And it doesn't need to go any further than that. Let's enjoy tonight and go back to complicated tomorrow."

Dear Reader,

The minute Dominic Mercado appeared on the page in *The Sinner's Secret*, I knew he was worthy of his own story. Especially when the fiery Meredith showed up beside him. I knew there was more to their story, and set against the glitz and glamour of Vegas nightlife, there was no doubt it would be a fun ride.

Dominic works hard to protect his heart of gold, even from Meredith, who's known him since they were both teenagers. He's carefully cultivated a reputation, one that's easy to view as excessive and self-serving. Which is exactly Meredith's opinion of him...until she learns his well-kept secret. Her view of him gets tossed upside down as she's forced to reevaluate everything she's ever thought of the infuriating and enticing man.

First impressions aren't always accurate. But it takes a strong person to admit that mistake, to reevaluate and truly view someone through honesty and forgiveness. I hope you enjoy reading Dominic and Meredith's story! I'd love to hear from you at www.kirasinclair.com or come chat with me on Twitter, www.Twitter.com/kirasinclair. And don't forget to check out Annalise Mercado's book, coming soon!

Best wishes,

Kira

KIRA SINCLAIR

———

SECRETS, VEGAS STYLE

HARLEQUIN

DESIRE

HARLEQUIN®
DESIRE™

Recycling programs for this product may not exist in your area.

ISBN-13: 978-1-335-73527-0

Secrets, Vegas Style

Copyright © 2021 by Kira Bazzel

All rights reserved. No part of this book may be used or reproduced in any manner whatsoever without written permission except in the case of brief quotations embodied in critical articles and reviews.

This is a work of fiction. Names, characters, places and incidents are either the product of the author's imagination or are used fictitiously. Any resemblance to actual persons, living or dead, businesses, companies, events or locales is entirely coincidental.

This edition published by arrangement with Harlequin Books S.A.

For questions and comments about the quality of this book, please contact us at CustomerService@Harlequin.com.

Harlequin Enterprises ULC
22 Adelaide St. West, 40th Floor
Toronto, Ontario M5H 4E3, Canada
www.Harlequin.com

Printed in U.S.A.

Kira Sinclair's first foray into writing romance was for a high school English assignment, and not even being forced to read the Scotland-set historical aloud to the class could dampen her enthusiasm...although it definitely made her blush. She sold her first book to Harlequin Blaze in 2007 and has enjoyed exploring relationships, falling in love and happily-ever-afters since. She lives in North Alabama with her two teenage daughters and their ever-entertaining bernedoodle puppy, Sadie. Kira loves to hear from readers at Kira@KiraSinclair.com.

Books by Kira Sinclair

Harlequin Desire

Bad Billionaires

The Rebel's Redemption
The Devil's Bargain
The Sinner's Secret
Secrets, Vegas Style

Harlequin Blaze

The Risk-Taker
She's No Angel
The Devil She Knows
Captivate Me
Testing the Limits
Bring Me to Life
Handle Me
Rescue Me

Visit her Author Profile page at Harlequin.com, or kirasinclair.com, for more titles.

You can also find Kira Sinclair on Facebook, along with other Harlequin Desire authors, at Facebook.com/harlequindesireauthors!

To KLT,
for always having my best interests at heart,
for pushing me to enjoy the things I've worked
for and for the kick-ass chicken parm.
Thank you for loving me and for being my muse!
Love you!

One

Dominic Mercado's cheek stung. But he supposed that was usually what happened when a woman slapped you across the face.

There were plenty of times in his life when he'd probably deserved to be slapped. But surprisingly enough, this was the first time it had actually happened. Which pissed him off for two very distinct reasons.

One, he didn't damn well deserve it. And two, Meredith Forrester, the gorgeous, dynamic, red-headed pain in his ass, was the one who'd done it.

Meredith's eyes glittered with rage, disappointment and self-righteous indignation. Clearly, she'd come to his club tonight looking for a fight. Which shouldn't intrigue him, but did. Especially considering he hadn't seen or spoken to her in probably close to two years.

Which raised the question, what the hell did she think he'd done?

Ultimately, it didn't matter. While sparring with Meredith and her sharp tongue had always been a favorite pastime, he had other, more important things to deal with tonight. Things that had already been delayed because his good friend Gray Lockwood had shown up.

Rather than meet her obvious aggression with some of his own, Dominic chose to flash her a slow, knowing grin. "Wonderful to see you, too, Meredith."

"Don't waste that smarmy smile and those bedroom eyes on me. I knew you when your face was covered with acne."

Dominic's grin only widened. God, this woman was a firecracker with energy to burn. The echo of that energy ignited deep in his gut. As it did every time she got close. If she'd been anyone else, Dominic would have seduced her a long time ago.

But she wasn't anyone else. She was Meredith, his sister's best friend. And forever off-limits.

"I see you haven't changed a bit. Still the stick-in-the-mud at every gathering."

She swatted her hand through the air, as if she could swipe away his words with the simple gesture. "Neither have you, if the information I'm hearing is true."

Considering he spent his nights running the hottest nightclub in Vegas, hobnobbing with the rich and famous, there was no telling what rumor she'd heard. His name was constantly being linked with some celebrity or another's. Only half of the stories were true. But for the life of him, he couldn't figure out what rumor might have crawled under her skin enough to warrant a trek into his world and a slap across the face.

Meredith avoided Excess like the place had the plague. She was too good for his club.

Dominic leaned into her personal space, purposely letting his gaze travel down the tight silver dress clinging to each and every curve of her body. "I frankly don't care what you've heard. But you're clearly not a little girl anymore, and I would have thought you'd outgrown listening to gossip a long time ago."

The maneuver, designed to make her uncomfortable, backfired on him. Meredith had obviously come dressed for the high-powered, partying VIP crowd that Excess cultivated. Her dress was like liquid metal, flashing and catching the lights whirling through the darkness around them. It skimmed the tops of her thighs, leaving the rest of her legs a bare, tempting invitation.

One he'd be stupid to accept.

Shoving at his shoulder, Meredith pushed him away. "I'm hardly playing at gossip, Nic. Why am I not surprised that you're not taking me seriously, though? You never have."

Nic laughed. "Please, you're serious enough for

the both of us, a walking, breathing example of the definition."

He'd bet all the money in his bank account that not once in all the years he'd known her had Meredith broken a rule or a law. She lived and breathed perfection and control.

That kind of existence would drive him crazy.

"And that, angel, has always been your problem." Reaching out, Dominic snagged the long, tempting tail of her red-gold hair and slid his fingers down it. "You wouldn't know fun if it bit you on the ass."

Jerking her head sideways, she pulled her hair from his grasp and glared up at him. "I know fun. I'm just not interested in sharing it with you."

And that was the biggest reason for him to take a nice, comfortable step away from her. To ignore the energy vibrating between them. Meredith wanted nothing to do with him.

She always had been smart.

"What I am interested in, though, is the tip I just received that you and this club are involved in human trafficking."

Shit.

Whatever he'd expected, it wasn't that. Dominic locked down his reaction. He had years of experience schooling his features. Having a physically and verbally abusive stepfather would teach you to hide your true thoughts.

With anyone else he might have turned on the charm as a distraction, but Dominic was well aware of Meredith's immunity to his effort. Instead, he went with direct. "Meredith, I thought you were smart enough to distinguish idle gossip from fact."

Her eyes blazed, and her luscious lips thinned. "Oh, I am. The tip came with proof. Proof the American media will lap up and delight in sending viral by tomorrow night."

Shit, damn, fuck. Meredith Forrester was a household name. Her career had broken through several years ago when she'd exposed a corruption scandal that went all the way to the vice president's office and then followed that up with a sex abuse scandal that rocked the music industry.

Whatever this proof was, it was solid enough to have Meredith storming into Excess at almost midnight to confront him. Dominic had always been aware there was a possibility his good deeds might come back to bite him on the ass. He just hadn't been ready for that to happen today.

Or for Meredith to be involved.

This was completely shitty timing. Because if Meredith would hurry up and leave, he was about to add another name to the list of young women who'd disappeared.

Not because he was involved in some illicit human trafficking ring, but because he, with the help of Gray Lockwood, Anderson Stone and Stone Surveillance, assisted abuse victims in disappearing.

The balls were all in motion for another woman, named Tessa, to disappear tonight. And while this diversion might suck for him, there was nothing he wouldn't endure in order to make sure she was safe.

Not to mention, if Meredith did run with the story, he might be under too much scrutiny to help Tessa tomorrow.

Meredith leaned closer, snarling, "Do you have any idea what this is going to do to your sister? Annalise is going to be devastated."

Dominic's stomach rolled. His sister was going to be more than devastated. She was going to be pissed. At least for a little while, until he could quietly explain things to her. Until then, she was just going to have to roll with the punches. And unfortunately, they both had plenty of experience with that.

"What happened to innocent until proven guilty?" Dominic asked, lifting a single, sculpted brow.

Meredith growled low, the rumbling sound sending shivers down Dominic's spine and making his lips twitch with humor.

"I'm a journalist, not a lawyer. If what I've seen is true, twelve of your peers will get to make that determination soon enough."

God, he wanted to bury his hands in the thick mane of her flame-and-gold hair, drag her up to his mouth and swallow that sound. He wanted to absorb her heat and taste all that sass and rigid control. Even now, he wanted to ruffle her feathers.

Unfortunately for him, he'd wanted Meredith for a very long time. Luckily, he had years of practice keeping his hands to himself. Because the last thing he needed was to mess with his little sister's idealistic, strict, perfectionist best friend.

Shaking her head, Meredith said, "I've always known you were a self-absorbed, hedonistic, excessive asshole only concerned with pursuing pleasure at any cost. But this... I never thought you capable of something truly despicable."

She might as well have spun around and planted one of her high heels in his solar plexus. Her words hurt a hell of a lot worse than his stinging jaw.

Trying to find his equilibrium again, Dominic pulled a deep draft of air into his lungs. Even in the face of what she'd just said, he had to fight to ignore the spicy, sweet scent of her perfume that came with it.

"As much as I'm enjoying this exchange... No, wait, that's not true. As much as this exchange has bored me, I appreciate you riding to my sister's rescue when neither she nor I required your assistance. I'm sure she'll be thrilled to learn of your crusade on her behalf. But I really can't stick around for act two, scene three. I have a nightclub to run."

And an abuse victim to protect.

He should have turned around and walked away, but despite everything, he couldn't stop himself from touching her. Dominic let his hand drop onto Meredith's shoulder and draw a light line down her arm to cup her elbow.

Her skin was soft and silky, warm beneath his touch. A tremor rocked through her body. He was smart enough to know she'd hate herself a little for the reaction, but he didn't care. He needed something from her other than animosity right now.

This was hardly the first time they'd played this game.

Leaning close, Dominic pressed a soft kiss to her cheek, as if they really were old friends, and murmured, "Be sure to let the bartenders know your fun is on me tonight." Pulling back, he gave her the wanton, devilish grin he'd perfected at fifteen. "Just don't do anything I wouldn't do," he admonished before walking away.

Don't do anything I wouldn't do. Meredith scoffed. That didn't leave much on the do-not-touch list. And even less than she'd thought if the information she'd received was true.

God, she didn't want it to be. She'd known Dominic a very long time. Since she'd met Annalise at the exclusive private school they'd all attended when they were teenagers. And while she'd never particularly liked him, she'd always understood why people—women in particular—flocked to him. The man was charm personified. He was smooth and sophisticated. Forever trying to make those around him laugh and smile. He excelled at spreading fun and excitement. Hell, he'd made a highly profitable business out of it.

But he liked to flirt. He had this uncanny way of making people feel special. She'd watched him do it for years and still couldn't seem to stop herself from falling for it sometimes.

Honestly, Meredith wasn't even sure it was entirely an act. Dominic genuinely enjoyed people and wanted to spread that enjoyment around.

It was dangerous, though, letting him close enough to suck you into that pretend world. Meredith knew it wasn't reality. Reality was the gritty, often nasty truth she investigated and exposed. Reality was being at the high-priced school because her mother was a teacher, not because her family could afford the exorbitant tuition. Reality was knowing she had to be top of her class in order to score a scholarship to college because her single mom couldn't pay for it. Duty, responsibility and expectation had been driving her for a very long time.

Dominic Mercado was the exact opposite of those things. The man was temptation personified. And she knew better than to fall for the act. Unfortunately, it wasn't always easy to remember.

However, she never would have expected him to go this far. But after spending the last several hours verifying the evidence file that had accompanied the anonymous email she'd received tonight…it looked like it might be true.

The information was damning. But human trafficking?

She'd originally come to Excess to confront Dominic, desperately looking for some other explanation. Maybe someone was framing him? Or maybe someone was using his club and he was unaware.

But one look at him and the acid-churning disappointment in her stomach had erupted into an unexpected anger that had caused her to lash out. Slapping him had been unwise, and she hated herself for the reaction.

But his complete lack of response when she'd finally gotten around to explaining why she was there had not given her the warm and fuzzies. Hell, his ever-present charming smile hadn't even slipped. Which only made her concerns grow.

Dominic didn't exactly have the most stellar reputation to begin with. He delighted in bending the rules just up to the point of breaking and always had. He was the guy who'd organized a party on the school grounds, complete with keg and bathtub punch, because it was the only space big enough to accommodate the entire student body. And he hadn't wanted anyone left out. He'd also stayed behind to take the heat when the cops had shown up with the principal in tow.

Even now, he had a reputation for throwing lavish parties, for engaging in shenanigans with high-profile VIPs and frankly for stirring up trouble. His name constantly appeared on gossip blogs. Videos of his parties went viral, and anyone who was anyone stopped by Excess to play when they were in town.

It was all a game to him. One she was aware he'd learned at a very young age. She understood where the need to test boundaries came from, but that didn't make it any easier to watch him do it.

Maybe he'd finally gone too far. Gotten involved in something he hadn't meant to?

It wasn't beyond the realm of possibility.

Up until she'd gotten that email, Meredith would have said Dominic was a lot of things, but an evil asshole wasn't one of them. If he was involved in human trafficking…

The heavy weight that had settled in her belly the minute she read those words grew. Meredith felt utterly sick.

Why was she taking this so personally?

Sure, Annalise was her best friend and important to her. And there was little doubt the information would devastate her. While Meredith could delay publishing the piece for a couple days, the threat that accompanied the email was clear. If she didn't publish it, someone else would.

Annalise idolized Dominic and always had. Meredith might not understand the dynamic of their relationship, but she didn't need to in order to recognize that it existed.

Sure, she was worried about her friend.

But that didn't explain what she'd just done.

Meredith shook her hand, still throbbing from where she's slapped Dominic.

Never in her life had she felt the need to lash out physically at another human being. And she was intelligent enough to realize her reaction was disproportionate.

And unacceptable.

Not that Dominic had appeared to care.

The man simply had the ability to make her react. He always had. And he delighted in pushing her buttons, mostly because he knew he could. Dominic Mercado frustrated her. While he gave the world the impression that he didn't give a damn about anything, she knew deep down in her bones that he did.

Because she'd seen the way he cared about Annalise.

Consequences didn't matter to him, which drove her up the wall. Because fear and consequences had been ruling her life for years.

She couldn't afford to take the cavalier attitude Dominic did. She didn't have a father with billions of dollars to bail her out and make sticky situations disappear. She didn't have power and money behind her. If she screwed up, she'd have lost her scholarship to the good school, her reputation, even now, her job.

With a sigh, Meredith contemplated stopping at the bar for a drink on her way out but decided a shot of tequila wasn't likely to help the situation. Excess wasn't exactly her kind of place, anyway. The loud music pulsing through the room reverberated inside her skull, adding to the headache already threatening at her temples.

Weaving through the strategically placed tables and gyrating bodies of the beautiful and restless, Meredith headed for the huge double doors at the opposite end of the large space.

She ignored everyone around her, uncaring and uninterested. Focused on her end goal of escape, Meredith was startled when a hand shot out, wrapping around her arm and pulling her to a stop.

"Beautiful girl, where are you going?"

Meredith's surprised gaze flew up to the face of a man she'd never seen before. He was handsome enough, but the glazed look in his eyes told her plenty about his state of mind. Ripping her gaze down, she took in his expensive suit, flashy watch and overpriced shoes. Drunk and entitled. This was why she didn't come to Excess.

Irritation quickly replaced shock. Meredith shook her arm, trying to dislodge his hold. Instead of taking the hint, the annoying idiot's fingers tightened.

Digging deep for a well of calm, Meredith said, "Let me go."

"Aw, don't be that way, gorgeous. I just wanna talk. Why don't you let me buy you a drink?" His words slurred, running together in a way that only increased her disgust.

The man used his height advantage and hold to draw her closer. A small frisson of anxiety shot through her body, but Meredith refused to let it flourish. She was surrounded by thousands of people, and this fool was simply too drunk on alcohol and a superiority complex to take a hint.

So she'd get direct.

Stepping into his personal space, Meredith started to reach for his crotch. Her plan was to grip and twist while she delivered a scathing rebuke. However, her hand never made it that far.

Instead, it was intercepted by another grip. Fingers intertwined with hers, and a jolt of electricity zinged up to her shoulder. Another arm wrapped around her waist, pulling her back against a warm, hard wall of solid male chest.

"This wasn't what I meant." Dominic's low,

smooth voice rumbled against her skin. Goose bumps erupted over her neck and chest. "You are truly remarkable. Five minutes alone and you manage to find trouble."

Those words were for her alone. To the guy in front of them, Dominic said, "I suggest the next time you set your hands on a lady in my club, you ensure she wants them there."

The man sputtered and tried to spout some excuse that was pointless and pitiful. Dominic ignored him, waving one of the security guards milling on the outskirts of the crowd over to them. "Please escort this gentleman off my property."

"But I'm here with some friends. They're my ride."

Dominic shrugged. "I suggest you call a cab or a rideshare. Or explain to them why you're being thrown out. Your choice."

The guard didn't even say a word; he simply gestured for the guy to walk ahead of him. Meredith watched as the man looked him up and down, calculated and decided there wasn't a snowball's chance in hell he could win that fight before doing as he'd been told.

Meredith expected Dominic to release her the minute the guy disappeared into the crowd, but he didn't. In fact, they stood there, together, in the middle of the crowded club, a moment of immobility amid the chaos.

Dominic's arm tightened around her waist, pressing her closer into his body. Meredith stood utterly still except for the pounding of her heart and the stuttered push and pull of oxygen inside her lungs.

She was afraid to move. Not because she was scared or worried. But because having his arm around her felt so damn good.

And she didn't want it to.

A huge part of her wanted to see his face, but the rest of her was glad she couldn't. She didn't want to know if he was pissed at her—because he had every right to be, from before, but she wasn't ready to apologize even if she knew she should.

She also didn't want to see that trademark smoldering, sexy bedroom expression that he'd perfected so long ago. Because right now, Meredith wasn't sure she'd be able to resist the pull of it.

And she'd hate herself if she gave in. Because while he had the ability to make everyone feel special with that look, the fact that she'd seen him use it liberally meant she couldn't afford to fall for it.

It wasn't real. That look wouldn't be about her.

And the weakest part of her wanted it to be.

Slowly, Dominic's hand slid across her belly, letting her go. Pushing her away, he spun her to face him.

While his voice had been pure sex in her ear, the expression on his face was anything but. And Meredith wasn't sure why that disappointed her.

"Are you all right?"

She swallowed, searching for the residue of anger and disappointment she'd walked in here with. Unfortunately for her, she couldn't find either.

"I'm fine now, and I was fine before you got involved. I'm a big girl and can take care of myself."

Dominic's jaw tightened, and his darker-than-sin eyes narrowed. Meredith tipped her head sideways, considering the obvious evidence of his anger.

"You're too smart a woman to say something so stupid. You better than most understand just how vulnerable women are. How many sexual assault stories have you covered? How many murders have you reported?"

"Too many."

Dominic opened his mouth to say something but snapped his jaw shut before any words slipped out. Shaking his head, he finally said, "I don't have time for this conversation right now. I take it back, no fun for you tonight. You're leaving."

"I didn't do anything wrong and you're kicking me out, too?"

"I'm kicking you out because I don't have time to babysit you."

"I don't need a babysitter and haven't in a very long time."

He didn't respond, but his eyebrows rose, challenging her statement, which pissed her off.

Dominic waved at another security staff member. A tall, slender woman dressed entirely in black strode over. She was gorgeous, with golden skin and deep brown eyes that seemed to be constantly searching. "Please escort Ms. Forrester to her vehicle and ensure she leaves."

It was Meredith's turn to sputter, which just irritated her more. It was frustrating to find herself at a loss for words. Hell, she made her living with them.

For the second time that night, Meredith watched Dominic dismiss her by walking away. Oh, her anger had resurfaced. She wanted to scream at him. However, she didn't, because not only would it have been undignified, but it wouldn't have made a bit of difference.

Instead, she let the woman lead her out of the club. It wasn't her fault, and Meredith didn't want to get the woman in trouble by causing more of a scene.

Besides, there was really no reason to stay.

Sliding into the deep leather seat of her SUV, Meredith started the car. She sat there for several seconds before putting it in gear and heading out of the busy lot.

She didn't want to do it, but she knew she needed to. Punching a button on her steering wheel, Meredith told her car to call her best friend.

And had to admit to feeling relief when all she got was voice mail.

"Annalise, call me. We need to talk."

Two

Dominic's body still hummed with energy. It had taken everything inside him not to lay that asshole who'd touched Meredith out on the shiny floor of his club.

Not a smart move. He paid good money for a security staff to handle these types of issues, and it wouldn't be good business for the owner to make that kind of scene. Everyone expected him to be the good-time guy, the one passing out shots and encouraging people to relax and enjoy.

Watching him flatten a guy on the floor would counter the devil-may-care attitude he'd purposely cultivated. But seeing that man's hand wrapped around Meredith's arm, holding her in place… It had been close.

Reputation was important. One thing Dominic guaranteed inside Excess was a safe environment for all his guests. Every staff member went through specialized training to be able to spot things like assholes slipping date-rape drugs into drinks, selling drugs, suicidal tendencies and of course signs of abuse.

He'd dealt with plenty of situations like Meredith's but never had such an immediate, visceral reaction.

But he didn't have time to dissect that right now.

Standing at the large window of his office overlooking the wide expanse of the club below him, Dominic took a deep, cleansing breath. He watched the people. Glitz, glamour and wild abandon. Dominic prided himself on creating a place where people felt safe and comfortable to simply be themselves. To let go and experience all the excitement life had to offer. Or at least the slice he could give them.

Reality didn't exist within the walls of Excess. Burdens, bad experiences, the weight of others' expectations…they all melted away. He made sure that every night was a party. An opportunity to forget pressure, depression and difficulties in a safe environment.

The best liquor, five-star cuisine, the latest music trends and hottest celebrities. Every guest at Excess could be a part of the exclusive Vegas elite, at least for a little while.

Jake slid up beside him. "Everything's set, boss."

Dominic watched the gyrating bodies and flashing lights for several seconds before giving a curt nod.

He might be hell-bent on creating a wonderland of excitement, but he wasn't oblivious to the dirty, nasty side that often tried to creep in to destroy utopia.

"We'll need to make a few changes."

"Because of the handprint on your cheek?"

Dominic tried to force out a smile. Jake was giving him hell, something they normally did with each other. But he really wasn't in the mood for that tonight.

He didn't want his friend to see, though.

Jake had been with Dominic since he'd first opened Excess eight years ago. They'd grown together, he a fledgling businessman and Jake newly retired from the military and trying to get into the security game. Now, Jake headed the entire security team for all Excess Inc. clubs.

But Jake's home base was Vegas. And when Dominic had approached him about being involved in protecting abused women, he hadn't hesitated to join in.

Though the walls of the office level were thick, Dominic could still hear the faint beat of music and feel the thump of it echoing through the soles of his feet. That small detail reminded him that no matter what difficulty faced you head-on, life still moved forward.

Tonight, they'd deal with Tessa and her situation. They'd get her someplace safe. Tomorrow would be soon enough to handle the mess Meredith was about to land in his lap.

"Yeah, but we'll talk about that later. Tessa needs

our undivided attention tonight. I need you to make the run with her."

Normally, Dominic escorted the women on the first leg of their journey. He did it not only to make sure they were safe, but because often by that time he'd built a rapport with them and they trusted him.

Luckily, Jake had sat in on a couple of his meetings with Tessa, so he wouldn't be a completely unfamiliar face.

"Do you think that's wise?"

"I don't think we have a choice."

Joker, hacker extraordinaire for Stone Surveillance, had pulled everything from Meredith's computer within minutes of his phone call to his friend Stone. What had been clearly obvious was that someone was watching Dominic. Closely. Given his confrontation with Meredith, he and Stone had agreed that Dominic couldn't afford the additional scrutiny.

"Tessa will be here in a couple hours."

"I got this," Jake said. "She'll be just fine."

God, Dominic hoped so. Tessa wasn't simply a battered woman who had come to him for help. She was an old friend of Meredith and Annalise's. Someone they'd gone to school with many years ago.

No doubt, it was the worst possible time for one of Meredith's own friends to disappear, especially under questionable circumstances. Or to be tied to him and Excess before her disappearance.

But there wasn't anything he could do about that. He'd been working for months to convince Tessa to leave her husband, Ben. And five days ago had been the straw that had finally broken through.

Leaning back against the edge of the desk, Dominic watched the churn of people beneath him.

And felt tired as hell. Usually, everything about running Excess energized him. Not tonight.

There were reports behind him to review. Papers to sign. He needed to approve a large liquor purchase for several of the locations. All minor details he normally handled without a thought. Right now, he didn't have the energy to deal with any of it.

The vision of Meredith crossing the floor of his club ghosted through his mind. That dress she'd been wearing…it was killer. And so out of her normal character. Not that he hadn't seen her in a cocktail dress before.

Another memory, one he'd shoved deep below the surface, reared up. Annalise and Meredith's senior year. Some formal dance at school. Several girls had come over to their house to get ready, including Meredith.

He could hear their giggles and chatter from down the hall, and the noise was like a spike inside his skull. He'd been cramming for an exam in one of his college classes—he couldn't even remember which one now. Desperate for a minute of quiet, he'd slipped outside onto the back patio.

The cool desert night had stretched before him, relief. The estate rolled out, his father's land all he could see. Not his, not theirs. Not that his father held his own success over Dominic's head, but he felt it—the drive to have something of his own. The need to start his life when it felt like he was simply standing still. He'd gone to college because it was expected. Hell, he was even good at it. But he hated every minute of it.

The gentle sound of water lapped against the side of the pool, and the soft drone of insects buzzed in his ears.

Something caught his attention, off to his left. Slowly, a shadow detached from the rest of the gloom. She stood there, staring out at the same vista of time and space. Her arms were wrapped around her own body, not fighting a chill, but holding herself close. He couldn't see her face, but her body language screamed loud and clear.

Meredith wasn't happy.

The need to wrap his arms around her and whisper that everything would be fine was almost overwhelming. It wasn't the first time he'd wanted to touch her.

But she wouldn't appreciate the gesture. Not from him.

Instead, Dominic stood right where he was, rocking up onto the balls of his feet as he shoved the palms that itched deep into his pockets.

"Why aren't you upstairs with the gaggle of girls?"

She whipped her head around, those pale blue eyes wide. For the flash of a second, Dominic saw fear in her expression and kicked himself for startling her.

Instinct had him closing the space between them. "I'm sorry, I didn't mean to scare you." That was the last thing he ever wanted to do.

Meredith's mouth twisted into a tight line. "You didn't."

Liar. He had, and he hated himself for putting that expression on her face.

Any other time he probably would have called her on the lie, using it to tease her and make her bristle at him like she always did. Her back going straight, pink flagging her cheeks and irritation glittering through those soul-stealing eyes. Tonight... for some reason she looked fragile. A word he never would have used to describe her before now.

He should turn around and leave. He knew it, deep down. But he didn't. Instead, he slid beside her, close enough to feel the heat seeping off her fragrant skin. The scents of vanilla and musk, a combination of sweet and darkness, teased his senses.

She shifted, her arms around her body tightening.

"What's wrong?" He shouldn't ask. He shouldn't care, but the words simply slipped out.

"Nothing."

This time, he wouldn't let the lie stand. "We both know that's not true. Tell me."

Meredith turned to look at him, the expression in her eyes punching him in the gut. A sheen of moisture threatened to spill over her gorgeous, sooty lashes.

He was going to kill someone. Whoever had made her cry.

She shook her head, refusing, even as the words tumbled out of her slick, shiny lips. "My date canceled. At the last minute." She groaned, dropping her head back to stare into the star-soaked sky. "It's stupid. I'm being stupid. He isn't someone I care about. We're not even dating."

"But it still hurts."

"Yeah, and listening to everyone talk about their dates and plans to sneak away to have sex in the back of some guy's car..." She shook her head.

Dominic had no idea why he did it. No, that wasn't entirely true. He did it because he'd been wanting to for years but knew he shouldn't. Knew it wasn't right.

Tonight, that didn't matter. Reaching for her, Dominic gently pulled her into his arms. Urging her up onto her toes, his mouth found hers. The kiss started quick. He'd meant it as nothing more than a soothing balm to her wounded pride. To assure her that she was pretty and desirable. Because she was.

But it quickly burned into more. The heat of her, the taste of her...it reached deep inside him and grabbed hold.

Never in his life had he felt like he was drowning without being anywhere near water. But that's how touching her made him feel. Lost, floating, gasping for breath.

Everything faded away but the taste and feel of her. Nothing and no one had ever made Dominic feel so...untethered and grounded at the same time.

And then she shoved him away.

The punch of her hands against his chest had him stumbling back.

"What are you doing?" Meredith gasped, staring up at him out of horrified eyes.

The pain of it burned almost as much as the searing perfection of that kiss. At least her tears had disappeared.

Pulling out his practiced grin, Dominic let his shoulders shrug with a careless gesture. "Didn't want you to feel left out, angel. You know I'm always available for some fun if you're disappointed about missing your own turn in the back seat of the family SUV." Leaning close, he whispered, "I promise you'd have a more enjoyable time with me, anyway. We both know I know what I'm doing."

Shoving at him again, Meredith didn't even bother responding. She'd simply walked away. Clearly, she wanted nothing to do with him then, and she wanted nothing to do with him now.

He hadn't thought about that night in a long time. Years. But for some strange reason his lips tingled, just as they had as he'd watched her leave.

Clenching his teeth, Dominic realized his fists ached from the tight balls they'd curled into. Deliberately releasing them, he shook them out.

Work. That's what he needed. Not some long-ago memory that meant nothing.

Turning back to his desk, Dominic was about to open a spreadsheet from the club in London when the phone in his pocket vibrated. Pulling it out, he rolled it over so he could see the screen.

And then sighed when he saw his sister's name illuminated.

Damn Meredith.

Meredith stared at the blinking cursor on her screen. Words scrolled through her head a mile a minute, but her fingers refused to type them out.

She just couldn't do it.

Damn Dominic.

Switching screens on her laptop, Meredith scrolled through the documents that had been sent to her. Articles about missing women that had been buried pages deep and barely given more than a blurb.

It was heartbreaking to see what little value the media had placed on these disappearances. Sometimes she was ashamed to be a part of the machine.

Whoever had sent her the information had done their homework. There were pictures from video surveillance cameras. Images of the women as they'd come and gone from Excess in the days and weeks leading up to their disappearances.

But that alone wasn't evidence enough that Dominic was involved. So the women had frequented his establishment…it was possible someone was using his business to identify and stalk victims. Excess made for perfect hunting grounds if you were a psychopath looking for lonely, impaired or extremely adventurous women who might be ripe for kidnapping.

And if that was all the email had contained, that's exactly the story Meredith would be writing. But it wasn't.

There were also photographs of Dominic getting into a sleek black car with a couple of the women.

Maybe he'd been sleeping with them. A sharp pain twisted through Meredith's gut.

Nope, she refused to let herself be jealous. Besides, it wasn't like Dominic to see the same woman more than once or twice, and each of them had been to the club multiple times. Just one more reason why she needed to keep her head focused on what was in front of her and not some phantom teenage fantasy she'd been fighting for years.

What bothered her more than anything right now was that if this story had involved anyone else, she wouldn't be hesitating. She'd checked sources. Verified the information. Enough to know that *something* was going on.

But Dominic was involved. And as much as she'd like to convince herself the reluctance to drag his name through the mud was entirely due to her relationship with Annalise…she knew deep down it wasn't.

Her gut told her the whole thing stunk and something about it just wasn't right. But the tiny voice in her head taunted her, suggesting she just didn't want to accept that Dominic could be involved.

Was she being stupid or pragmatic?

God, she didn't even know. And that was the whole problem with Dominic. While her brain screamed danger whenever he was close, the rest of her wanted to grab the back of his neck and kiss the hell out of him.

Maybe if she did, she could prove to herself that their one kiss—her first kiss—hadn't been as earth-shattering as she remembered.

She simply needed to find something that proved she was right.

Dominic hadn't been questioned in any of the missing-person cases. Which meant he hadn't come forward.

Why not?

It was possible the officers working the case hadn't found the evidence that had been sent to her. The cases had all been assigned to different officers, which probably complicated things.

But that did make her wonder, why hadn't the information been sent to the police? Or the DA? Why a reporter? Why her? Sure, she had a reputation for uncovering corruption and taking down people with money and connections.

But…something about it felt wrong. Her connection to Annalise's family was well-known.

Maybe someone was hoping to torpedo Dominic in the media before the police got involved? Convict him in the court of public opinion?

Could her informant have a personal ax to grind?

She needed to find someone with an IT background who could help her identify whether the photographs were doctored. Unfortunately, she didn't know anyone with that kind of skill set. But she did know someone who had access to that kind of technology.

Annalise managed Magnifique, the family casino,

and if anyone had access to high-tech gadgets and the brainpower to use them, it was her security staff. That place had an eye-in-the-sky tech team the CIA would weep to possess.

Meredith had threatened Dominic with telling Annalise, but so far, her friend hadn't called her back. Which wasn't entirely out of the ordinary if she was busy handling an issue at the casino.

Meredith hadn't exactly been looking forward to the phone call, anyway. With a sigh, Meredith picked up her phone and dialed her best friend again.

This time, Annalise answered. "Meredith, you're up late."

She was—it wasn't often that she made it past midnight before falling asleep. But tonight, between her encounter with Dominic and the visual of those pictures spinning in her head…she couldn't rest.

"Yeah, listen. I need your help."

Annalise didn't respond right away, which could have meant she was surprised Meredith was asking for help, but it also could have meant she was busy and distracted. Like her brother, her business kept her up late at night. "Okay, with what?"

"I need help identifying if some photographs have been doctored. I figured you had people on staff who could probably do that kind of thing."

"I do…is this for a story?"

Regret twisted through Meredith. She really didn't want to be the source of conflict between Annalise and her brother. But she had no choice. Annalise needed to know what was going on, especially if she was going to help.

With a deep sigh, Meredith said, "Yeah. I'll tell you about it when I get there."

This wasn't the kind of conversation she wanted to have over the phone.

Three

The night just wouldn't end. Dominic stood at the smoked glass in his office and stared down at the twisting, gyrating bodies beneath him.

Behind him, his cell phone vibrated against the top of his desk. Glancing over, he saw Gray Lockwood's name scroll across the screen. He'd been waiting for this call.

"I hear we have a problem."

No niceties or smoke up his ass. Gray was as to-the-point as Dominic was. One of the things he liked best about the guy. "Yeah, we do."

There was a pause at the other end before his friend said, "Explain."

No doubt Joker had filled Gray in on some of the information, but Gray wanted to hear the particulars from Dominic. "A reporter—" Dominic left out that the reporter was an old family friend "—has a story tying me and Excess to the disappearance of five women over the last eighteen months."

A string of curse words flowed through the phone.

Dominic wanted to add his own, but that wouldn't help anything. Instead, he said, "I couldn't agree more."

"Any chance we could kill the story?"

Gray's question was a logical one. The easy solution. If the reporter were anyone besides Meredith, that might have been a possibility. But he knew firsthand just how straight an arrow his sister's best friend was.

"Not this one. She isn't interested in bribes or quid pro quo."

"Any chance we could tell her the truth and bring her in?"

Again, if it had been anyone other than Meredith, he would have been tempted. It might have been valuable to have someone in the media on their side. Someone who could bury and spin stories when they needed it.

But for several reasons, he didn't want Meredith anywhere near what he and Stone Surveillance had going. The chief reason being that dealing with abusers was dangerous.

"No." Dominic didn't bother with an explanation or excuse. "She can't be involved."

Gray grunted but didn't question Dominic's edict.

"Well, maybe we can throw a little weight at her and get her to walk away."

"I doubt it. She's got a reputation for being ruthless when it comes to getting the story. And not easily intimidated."

"It's worth a shot, at least."

Dominic shrugged even though he knew Gray couldn't see him. "Whatever makes you feel warm and fuzzy, but trust me, she isn't going to let this drop."

Gray made another sound, this one closer to an *aha* of understanding. "You two have history. This is personal for her."

Oh, it was personal all right, but not the way Gray thought. "She's my little sister's best friend. I've known Meredith since I was fifteen."

"Let me guess, best friend never liked you?"

It was Dominic's turn to grunt. "Let's just say that while Annalise and Meredith have been joined at the hip since middle school, there's never been any love lost for me."

Meredith's expression of horror as she'd pushed him away after that kiss played through his mind for the second time tonight. Accompanied by all the verbal jabs she'd made at his expense over the years.

"Her opinion of me is pretty low."

"Too bad you didn't employ that bad-boy charm and seduce her out of her panties when she was sixteen. Women always have a soft spot for their first."

"Shut up, man." Dominic wasn't about to admit

that Meredith was the one woman he'd never had a shot in hell of seducing.

Gray laughed, the sound a little too gleeful for Dominic's liking. "Oh, it's like that."

Dominic couldn't hide the frost in his voice as he said, "I don't know what you mean."

"Sure you don't, but I'll let that one slide for now. What about your sister? Could she convince the friend to drop the story?"

Dominic had thought for certain when his phone rang earlier that Meredith had left Excess and gone straight to Annalise. But his sister had been calling about their father, not the potential mess he was about to land in.

He really didn't want to drag Annalise into this. And telling her about the article meant he'd probably have to come clean about his extracurricular activities.

He didn't want Annalise involved in this any more than he wanted Meredith close to it.

"Probably not. She wouldn't ask Meredith to bend her principles. She knows how important those damn principles are to Meredith." Dominic heard the frustration and irritation in his voice but couldn't seem to curb it. "I really don't want to talk to Annalise about any of this if I don't absolutely have to."

Gray hummed. Considering his line of work, no doubt the other man understood Dominic's reluctance to involve the women in his life.

Not that Meredith was in his life.

"We'll start with a phone call to Ms. Forrester. Let's see where that gets us. We can go from there."

Dominic grunted again. He wasn't entirely convinced that phone call wouldn't result in another visit from Meredith. And, frankly, his jaw still stung a little.

He was about to end the call when Gray's final words stopped him. "Dominic, don't worry."

That was easy for Gray to say. He was all the way in South Carolina, far from Vegas and the shitstorm that was brewing. But what else could he say? "Yeah."

"We planned for this. We knew it was likely to happen at some point."

They had. That many women disappearing with connections to Excess, one of them was bound to get traced back to his club. But that was different. They'd made contingency plans for if the police investigated one of the disappearances. They'd never discussed what would happen if they started tracing *all* of them back to Dominic's place.

"Trust me, Nic, we have your back."

He absolutely trusted Gray and the rest of the team at Stone Surveillance.

He had to. Right now, he didn't have much choice.

"All right. Let me know what you come up with."

Meredith's phone rang. She looked down at the screen as she was driving. *Unknown.*

Normally, she didn't bother to answer calls from people she didn't know, but given the current situation… She hit the button on the steering wheel to connect the call.

"Hello?"

"Meredith Forrester?" an unfamiliar male voice asked.

"Yeeees," she responded, reluctant and weary. It was too late—or early, depending on your perspective—for telemarketers. Whoever this was, it probably wasn't good.

"This is Anderson Stone."

Meredith's hands jerked, and the car swerved partway into the opposite lane. She knew exactly who Anderson Stone was. Everyone did. Years ago, his arrest for the murder of the son of a prominent Southern family had gone viral. The story had gripped the nation, not just because of the powerful families involved, but also because of the speed and secrecy surrounding Anderson's incarceration.

And that sensationalism had only returned tenfold when he was released and it subsequently came out that he'd had very good reasons for his actions— he'd been defending his childhood friend after she was raped.

Stone was a powerful man in his own right. Wealthy, successful. She'd read an article saying that he'd opened a business of his own, along with sitting on the board at Anderson Steel.

So why the hell was he calling *her*?

"What can I do for you, Mr. Stone?"

"Just Stone. I wanted to talk to you about Dominic Mercado."

Dominic? She had no idea Dominic even knew Anderson Stone. Although it wasn't like she had reason to know all Dominic's friends.

"What about him?"

"You're making a mistake."

Shaking her head, Meredith pulled over onto the shoulder of the road. Something told her she was going to need to give this conversation 100 percent of her concentration.

"Excuse me?"

"Looks can be deceiving, Ms. Forrester. I recognize that the photographs and information sent to you might appear damning."

"There's no might about it."

Obviously, Dominic had contacted his powerful friend in the hopes that his connections could convince her to let the whole thing go. Irritation and disappointment curled through Meredith's belly. She should have known Dominic wasn't above a little strong-arming.

Unfortunately for him, Meredith wasn't as fragile as she looked. And she definitely wasn't willing to drop a story with such serious implications.

She was about to say just that when Stone's words actually penetrated the fog of emotion. She'd never told Dominic exactly what she'd received—or that the files included photographs.

"How do you know I have photographs?"

A soft chuckle flowed through the connection. "Let's just say I only employ the best."

"You hacked into my computer?"

"No, I didn't say that."

He didn't need to. That was the only way anyone could know about the photographs.

"Stay out of my computer, and while you're at it, tell your friend to stay away from me, too."

"Which one? From what I understand, you and Dominic have a history."

The way he said it made heat flare through Meredith's body. And it wasn't all anger. "I don't know what he told you, but we most certainly don't have *that* kind of history."

This time Stone didn't bother muffling his laughter. "From what I hear, you went to him. And left a nice impression on his cheek. That tells me you care…and you don't really want to write this story."

Meredith really hated feeling at a disadvantage, and right now, in this conversation, she felt like Anderson Stone held all the cards. And she had none.

Because he was right. She didn't want to write the story. "That won't from me from doing it."

"Which is exactly what he said you'd say."

Meredith needed to wake up. She was damn good at interviewing people, so she needed to get her head out of her ass and into the game. This was an opportunity to gather whatever intel she could…because obviously she'd struck some nerves if Anderson Stone was willing to give her a call in the middle of the night and issue a, what…? A warning?

"Since you've obviously seen the information, you know it isn't just damning. It's pretty airtight."

"Is that why you haven't started writing a piece on it? Because it's so airtight?"

Of course he'd know that. They'd hacked her computer, which didn't have a draft because every time she tried to put words on the page, her brain froze.

Damn him. "No, it's because I'm a decent human being and a good journalist. I won't print something like this, something that could completely destroy another person's life, without double- and triple-checking everything."

This time Stone's laugh was full of derogatory disbelief. "Excuse me if I find that hard to believe. I've dealt with quite a few people from the media before, and in my experience not many of them have a single shred of integrity."

"Well, I'm not everyone. I take my job and my responsibility as a journalist seriously."

"Excellent." Stone's voice was full of authority as he said, "Then forget you ever saw those images."

He might be a high-profile businessman, used to people following his orders, but she wasn't one of his employees. "I won't do that."

A sigh escaped, the sound of it rushing through her and making her feel bone-deep exhausted all of a sudden. "Dominic said you'd say that, too. Look, I can promise you it isn't what it appears to be."

"And I'm just supposed to take your word for it? Someone I've never met?"

"Isn't that what you're doing by accepting those photographs at face value?"

Meredith hated that he had a point. "Who said

anything about accepting them at face value? Although you have to admit, the evidence is hard to ignore. So far all you've given me is some cryptic statement that looks can be deceiving. I need something more concrete."

"I can't give you that."

"Then I think this conversation is finished."

"Ms. Forrester, you strike me as a woman who values honesty. You've built a career out of exposing those that hide, cheat, steal and defraud."

Meredith answered slowly, trying to pinpoint where he was going and where the trap was. Because he was clearly setting one. "I am."

"Then accept this as truth—if you publish a piece tying the disappearance of those women to Dominic and Excess, you're going to endanger a lot of people. People who deserve to be safe."

The sincerity in his voice was difficult to ignore, but at the end of the day, he still hadn't offered her anything solid. "That doesn't mean anything to me, Mr. Stone. What exactly are you trying to say?"

"I'm not trying to say anything, I'm being as plain as I possibly can. People's lives will be disrupted. Their safety, security and sanity will be in danger. Not to mention the turmoil Dominic and his family, including Annalise, will experience. I understand you feel a need to expose potential criminal activity."

"I feel a responsibility to help these women who've disappeared. From what I've seen so far, no one else appears to care that they're missing."

"Oh, I assure you, there are plenty of people

who care. Were you aware that I'm part owner of Stone Surveillance, an investigative company out of Charleston?"

She'd known he owned a business, but not what kind. "No, I wasn't. How is that relevant?"

"I'm just pointing out that the police aren't the only ones who can assist in these types of cases."

"Are you telling me that your company, from halfway across the country, is handling multiple missing-person cases in Las Vegas?"

"What would you do if I said yes?"

Meredith tilted her head and considered that for several seconds before answering. "I'd say you suck at your job, considering all the women are still missing. And I'd also say that sounds like a line of BS you're spouting to help protect your friend."

Another soft chuckle ghosted down the line. "He told me you were stubborn, straight as an arrow and wouldn't listen."

Dominic had said that about her? "Perhaps you should have believed him."

"Oh, I did, but just like you, felt I needed to try. I won't take up any more of your time. I'll simply ask that you seriously consider what I've said and think long and hard about the consequences for writing your piece."

"And I'd tell you that the consequences for not writing my piece seem to outweigh those for writing it right now."

Stone grunted, said, "Think about what I've said," and then the connection died.

Meredith sat for several moments, staring at the blank screen of her phone. Anderson Stone's words spun through her head, making her question, but also pissing her off all over again.

He'd called her to throw his weight around. To try and intimidate her and influence her decisions. It wasn't the first time that had happened in her career, but somehow this time felt more personal.

Because Dominic had asked him to. His own tactics hadn't worked, so he'd called in reinforcements.

If there was one thing she hated, it was someone with money thinking they could influence others to do what they wanted simply because they had power. While Dominic had never struck her as that type, this was irrefutable proof that he was.

Which left her disappointed. Again.

One thing was certain, she was even more determined now to get to the bottom of this. She needed to know the truth.

Four

"Excuse me?" Meredith cringed at the utter anger in Annalise's voice. Mostly because she was afraid her friend might point that anger in her direction, since she was the messenger.

"Look, I know this is hard to swallow."

"Meredith, we're talking about Dominic here. Sure, he can be a charming asshat. And he definitely has a reputation for playing fast and loose with women…but doesn't that negate what's in front of us? Dominic isn't the kind of man who has to resort to abducting women in order to get them to sleep with him. Hell, all he has to do is flash that sexy bad-boy grin and women line up to throw their panties at him."

This time Meredith's cringe had nothing to do

with Annalise's tone. Because she wasn't wrong. Dominic didn't need to do anything more than crook his finger for most women to go breathless in his presence.

It was disgusting to watch. And Meredith had watched it plenty.

Annalise shook her head. "There has to be another explanation."

Anderson Stone's words, eerily similar to Annalise's, rang through her mind. "I want there to be, but…" She let the sentence drop between them.

Annalise's mouth tightened into a grim line. "So what do you need from me? You asked for IT help, right?"

"I want to make sure none of the photographs have been doctored. Do you have someone on staff who could analyze them?"

"Absolutely."

Annalise spun away, snatched up the phone on her desk and said, "Send Mav over. I have a special project I need his help on."

Dropping the phone back into the cradle, Annalise crossed her arms over her chest. She pulled in a deep breath. Meredith watched thoughts flit across her friend's face.

Pure sadness settled at the forefront. "This can't be true, Meredith."

She wanted to tell her best friend that of course it wasn't. Dominic was Annalise's rock. Her protector. And not just in a big-brother, scare-off-potential-creepy-dates kind of way.

Dominic was the sort of big brother who'd always been around, despite the fact that he was several years older than they were. He was a fixture in Annalise's life. He'd attended every dance recital, track meet and cheer competition Annalise had ever participated in.

Which had always struck Meredith as a little out of character. Dominic had a laid-back, out-for-himself-and-his-own-pleasure kind of attitude. To see him place Annalise's happiness over his own had been...confusing.

Because she'd watched him flippantly dismiss most everyone else in his life as unimportant—women, friends, it didn't matter.

Or at least that's how it had appeared to her. The man was frustrating in so many ways—then and now.

Meredith wanted desperately to tell Annalise that everything would be okay. But she simply couldn't.

And a couple hours later, she was glad she hadn't given in to the compulsion.

"You're certain," Annalise asked, her words sharp.

The big guy sitting at the computer terminal turned apologetic eyes their way. "Yes, ma'am. These photographs were pulled from different sources, but none of them have been altered."

Dammit, Dominic.

"I'm going to kill him." Annalise spun away, pacing for several steps before yanking a drawer in her desk open and picking up her purse from the depths inside.

She was stalking across the room before Meredith could take a breath. Rushing behind her, she tried to keep up. "Where are you going?"

"To yell at my brother."

This was not going to go well.

If she was smart, she'd let Dominic and Annalise work through this on their own. But for some reason Meredith felt responsible.

There was also a part of her that hoped that when confronted with Annalise's anger and disappointment, Dominic would offer up an explanation for everything.

Dominic stared through the large wall of windows, looking out over the grinding bodies and party going on below him. The soundproof glass kept the noise out, although the picture of decadence and the twirling lights still managed to invade.

"Everything's ready, Nic."

Dominic turned, acknowledging Jake.

"She's ready to go?"

Jake nodded. "Considering what's going on, I'm glad you didn't back down from helping her. A lot of men would've protected their own skin."

Dominic shrugged. "I'll be fine." He hoped. "But Tessa wouldn't be. The next time he might not just crack her ribs and fracture her wrist."

Images he tried to keep at bay flashed across his mind. Dominic stood still, letting them flow like water. Years of experience had taught him that when the memories came, the only way to deal with them was not to fight. To just let them come, along with the sorrow, anger and utter frustration.

Jake's voice broke through the memories. "She wants to see you before we go."

Steam rolled from the tailpipe of the sleek car, billowing around it before melting into the air. Opening the back door, Dominic slid into the seat of the limo.

"How are you holding up?"

The woman across from him gave him a barely there half smile. "I'm okay." Blonde and beautiful, she projected an air of delicate fragility. In another life, he might have been interested in her.

The moment that thought crossed his mind, the vision of Meredith standing in front of him, eyes blazing with fury and determination, pushed it out of the way.

Reaching across the seat, Dominic grasped her hand and squeezed. "I promise, he won't find you."

"You can't make that promise."

That's where she was wrong. But Tessa didn't let him respond.

"Ben's powerful and connected. He has a lot of money, and he thinks of me as an object. Just something else he bought and paid for, like his mansions, cars and jet."

Dominic gripped her hand harder. "And you have several very powerful men protecting you. With a lot more resources. Ben will never find you."

Beneath his hold, Tessa's hands trembled. Her

skin was icy. There was nothing he could do or say to take away the fear. Only time could do that.

A bang on the hood of the car made her jump.

"It's time to go." Leaning across the space between them, Dominic pulled her into the shelter of his body and gave her a hug. She felt so frail. "You're going to be fine. More than that, you're going to be happy and safe."

Tessa squeezed back, using more strength than he'd thought she possessed. "Thank you," she whispered before letting go.

Dominic climbed from the car, double-checked the arrangements with Jake and then walked back into the club. He didn't bother looking back as the car drove away. His team would let him know once Tessa was settled into the first leg of her journey. It would be at least a day before she reached her final destination and took on the new identity Joker had prepared for her.

Slipping through the darkened corridors of the executive offices, Dominic surveyed the evidence of the life and business he'd built. He was proud of all he'd accomplished, but he was most proud that he'd done it on his own with absolutely no help from his father.

Walking back into his office, Dominic took up a position at the windows again, staring at everything he'd created and built.

He should be down there right now, not simply because it was good business for his employees to see him, for his customers to interact with him and for him to have an immediate finger on the pulse of what was happening within his club. But because being seen down there right now might offer an alibi he'd need later.

And that pissed him off.

But he couldn't make himself go down. He didn't want to be friendly or charming. And he definitely didn't want to be hit on by women who only saw him as a fleeting conquest or a means to something they wanted.

Which was why he was still standing there, hands in his pockets, staring down at the people around him enjoying the fruits of his labor when the door to his office swung open. The resounding snap of the metal knob hitting the wall echoed through the space.

Along with Annalise's pissed-off voice.

"Dominic, what the hell have you been doing?"

Meredith trailed behind Annalise as she stalked through the empty hallway of the executive offices of Excess.

Excess was his flagship, but he owned several other clubs across the globe—LA, Atlanta, Seattle, Miami, Rio, London, Paris. All around them was the evidence that while people partied their lives away downstairs, real business happened upstairs. Although all the offices were empty at this time of night.

The hallway, wide and open, led straight down to a set of double doors. On either side were multiple offices, glass soaring from about waist-high to the ceiling. The glass offered a sense of privacy while still leaving the space open. Modern and collaborative. The furnishings were expensive and the workstations inside each of the offices completely unique in their configuration and decoration. Obviously, each person was encouraged to make their office their own.

But Meredith didn't care about any of that. As much as the other offices were open, the one at the very end was closed. Oh, there was glass on either side of the heavy double wooden doors, but it was frosted, not clear.

The king obviously required privacy while he demanded openness from those around him.

Meredith had never been inside Dominic's inner offices. Sure, she'd been downstairs at the club a handful of times over the years, but never into the inner sanctum. And she'd liked it that way.

Her friend, however, appeared perfectly familiar with the surroundings. And she had no problem ignoring the pretty clear message that Dominic's office was off-limits. She didn't even bother knocking before barging through the double doors.

"Dominic, what the hell have you been doing?" Annalise didn't exactly wait for a welcome, either, before launching into her attack.

Meredith went with a different approach. She eased inside, quietly shutting the doors behind her.

Dominic stood on the far side of the massive office, hands in the pockets of his perfectly tailored suit pants. At some point he'd abandoned the matching jacket, tossing it over an overstuffed chair in the corner. The sleeves of his crisp white shirt were rolled halfway up his arms, revealing corded muscles and the beautifully intricate black-and-gray tattoo sleeves that decorated both.

Those were new. At least, he hadn't had them when they were younger and he'd cavorted in the pool with his sister while Meredith studiously tried not to notice the hard outline of his muscled body.

For some reason Meredith wanted a closer look at the art permanently marked on his body. She wanted to run her fingertips over the dark lines and feel the heat of his skin beneath her touch. She wondered what they meant. What part of him they represented.

But that wasn't really what mattered right now.

Apparently, she was still failing at ignoring the pull of him.

Dominic didn't even acknowledge his sister before turning his dark gaze straight to Meredith. A single eyebrow quirked up in disdain. "I see you finally tattled."

"Oh, grow up," she bit out.

A knowing smirk played at the corners of his lips.

"I don't see how any of this is funny," Annalise barked. "Seriously, Nic. What the hell is going on? Tell me it isn't true."

Dominic held her gaze for several seconds, his other eyebrow drawing up to join the first, as if to say, *see what a mess you've caused?*

She hadn't done this, dammit.

Narrowing her own gaze, Meredith stood her ground, refusing to flinch. Even if she did feel slightly guilty for whatever drama was about to go down between the siblings. She hadn't forced him into interacting with those women. She'd simply shed a light on the truth.

Or what appeared to be the truth. Even if something in her gut still left her feeling off.

Dominic was the first to look away, but somehow she didn't find any satisfaction—or relief—in that.

Crossing the room, he reached for his sister, gripping both her shoulders in his hands. He tried to pull her in close, but Annalise was having none of that. She resisted, keeping the distance between them as she stared up into her brother's dark green eyes.

"Oh, no, you don't. Don't try and pull that shit. This is not something a brotherly hug is going to fix. I don't have a skinned knee or a broken heart from an idiot boyfriend. Answer me, Nic."

With a shrug, Dominic dropped his hands. "I would, but I don't know exactly what she said."

Annalise's foot started tapping the ground. A loud, impatient staccato that matched Meredith's own frustration. "Stop playing word games," Annalise growled.

"Fine. Whatever Meredith has told you—" his gaze flicked her way again for the barest second "—or shown you, I can assure you it isn't what it appears."

"That's what I thought. And then I had someone on my IT team evaluate the photographs, and without a doubt he said they haven't been doctored."

Meredith stayed in the background, ever watchful

as the siblings engaged. She wanted—no, needed—
to see the expression on Dominic's face as he spoke
to his sister about what was going on.

She'd learned over the years that often the most
important thing an interviewee revealed had nothing to do with the words they spoke. It was body
language. Reaction. Or what they were careful not
to say.

Meredith had no doubt Dominic possessed the ca-
pability to lie to her face, but she wasn't as certain he
had the capacity to lie to his sister in the same way.

Letting out an exhausted sigh, Dominic finally
said, "That's because they're not altered."

What Meredith hadn't expected was for him to
pretty much incriminate himself.

Five

From the minute Meredith had walked into his club and confronted him, Dominic had known this conversation was inevitable. Maybe it was lucky that it had waited until Tessa was safely away.

Because if either woman had seen their friend lurking in the back lot of Excess before disappearing...

Dominic really didn't want to pull either Annalise or Meredith into the middle of any of this.

And not simply because the women he helped were running from dangerous situations. But because obviously there was someone out there on the hunt to hurt him.

What other explanation was there for someone anonymously providing incriminating evidence to

Meredith? Someone was playing a dangerous game, and Meredith was simply a pawn on the board. And now she'd dragged Annalise into it.

Dominic wanted nothing more than to take both of them out of the game so neither could be hurt— or used against him.

Easier said than done, considering both women were stubborn, brilliant and loyal.

"What do you mean, they're not?" Annalise demanded.

"I mean the photographs are real."

Annalise stared at him for several seconds before slowly asking, "You're admitting you were one of the last people known to have seen at least four women that have gone missing?"

"I'm admitting that all the women were patrons at my club. It's not out of the realm of possibility that I interacted with them."

"Date stamped the night they went missing?" For the first time since they'd both come in, Meredith stepped into the circle of the conversation. He'd wondered how long it would take for her nature to kick in.

Meredith had always been inquisitive, unable to let something go once she'd started pulling at a thread until she'd unraveled the entire ball of string.

"This is more than you simply being in the same general area, and you know it. You weren't just sitting beside or standing near these women. In several of the photographs, you were actively engaged with them. In one your arm is around her, her head bent to yours like you're part of an intimate conversation."

Dominic let a knowing smile play across his lips. His gaze darted across Meredith's face, taking in her pursed mouth and the crinkles of disdain at the edges of her eyes.

Her opinion of him hurt. He didn't want it to, but it did. Which was probably why he felt the need to hit back, just a little. "Jealous, angel?"

"Hardly. And don't call me angel."

Dominic couldn't help but think of Meredith that way. It had been his silent nickname for her since they were young. That's always how he'd seen her… the perfect angel, pristine. Untouchable.

And the name was a reminder to keep his hands to himself. Because his life had been a messed-up hell for a long time. And had no room for an angel in it.

Right now, he needed that reminder more than usual. Standing in the center of his domain, flashing lights swirled across Meredith's pale skin, and fire burned through her gaze. Fisted hands on her hips, feet spread wide apart, she reminded him so much of the avenging version of his nickname for her.

She was gorgeous. Fierce. Dynamic.

Annalise stepped into his line of sight, blocking off the tempting view. "Dominic, this doesn't make any sense."

Being forced to stare into his sister's unhappy gaze wasn't any better. The look of devastation and confusion ripped through the center of Nic's soul.

He'd seen that same expression on her face before, when their stepfather had put it there.

Closing the gap between them, he grasped Annalise's hands and brought her close. "Lise, you know me. I'm not capable of what Meredith is suggesting."

Meredith made a protesting sound in the back of her throat, but Dominic ignored her.

God, he wanted to tell her the truth. But he couldn't. Not if he wanted to keep her safe. Annalise would jump into this with both feet, not only to help the women, but also to protect him.

And he didn't want her putting herself in harm's way for his sake. It was his job to protect her, not the other way around. He'd failed at it before—he wouldn't fail at it right now.

"I know it looks bad, and I can't give you another explanation. But I promise you, I did not harm those women, nor am I responsible for placing them in a situation that might endanger them. I need you to believe me."

He stared deep into his sister's eyes, willing her to see the truth. To accept what he was saying without asking questions he couldn't answer. Not without placing her in jeopardy.

He watched the struggle cross Annalise's face. Fact weighed against instinct. It was such a difficult thing to ask of her. Of anyone.

Her gaze raced over his features, searching for a clue that would tip the scales one way or the other. After several seconds that felt like years, she finally pulled in a deep breath and let it out with an audible sigh.

"I don't understand, Nic, but you're right. I've known you my whole life and possibly know you better than you do yourself. This isn't something you're capable of doing. Which is what I've been saying from the moment Meredith brought the information to me."

Closing his eyes with relief, Dominic whispered, "Thank you." His one biggest fear was that Annalise wouldn't be able to see past appearances and trust what she knew.

Hearing her say she accepted his explanation gave him the shot of strength he was going to need to get through what came next.

Because he had no doubt Meredith wasn't going to be as easily convinced. And she had a public forum at her disposal.

Oh, he wanted to be angry at the prospect of her using it against him. But, honestly, he didn't blame her. In fact, he admired her tenacity…it would just be more convenient if it wasn't aligned against him at the moment.

Not simply because it was going to make his own life difficult, but because if she did go public with the story, she was going to find herself an unwitting piece in a dangerous game she didn't need to be playing.

"Whatever's going on, Nic, please be careful. Someone's gunning for you."

"I'm well aware."

Reaching out, Annalise set the cool cup of her palm against the edge of his jaw. "If I can do anything, let me know."

"Thanks," he answered, although he had no intention of taking her up on the offer. At least he could keep Lise far from whatever was happening.

Turning, his sister slipped out of the office. He listened to the muted sound of the heels of her shoes hitting the floor as she disappeared.

Meredith didn't follow, at least not right away. She stood in the center of his office, her head tilted sideways and her mind clearly working overtime to unravel the hidden meaning of what had just transpired.

God, her mind was so attractive.

"I'm not so easily swayed," she finally said.

Dominic huffed out a laugh. "I never expected you would be. I'm quite familiar with who you are, Meredith. And I'm going to guess that whoever forwarded you those photographs is as well."

He'd said the words in the hopes that they might make her stop and think.

The corner of her lips twitched with the hint of a self-deprecating smile. "Oh, I'm well aware that I'm being used, Dominic. But that doesn't negate the validity of the information I've been provided. Even a pawn has an important role to play in the game."

"This isn't a game, Meredith. It's my life."

Meredith's body stiffened. "Do you think I don't realize that? But we're not just talking about your life, Nic. The lives of five women hang in the balance as well."

"They don't."

She shook her head. "How can you be so certain?"

That was a question he couldn't answer. Not without dragging her even deeper into this mess. While he'd never made Meredith any promises to protect her, he'd do it, anyway. Even if he had to protect her from herself.

Stone was currently having a conversation with some of the editors that Meredith typically worked with. While it irritated the hell out of him to use those contacts, he was willing to do it to try and stop the spread of any potential story.

Hopefully, by morning Meredith would find that the outlets interested in her story would be limited. For now, he was willing to give Stone some time to work.

But that wouldn't stop Dominic from trying to reason with her still. "Why are you letting yourself be used if you know that's what's happening?"

She shrugged. "I don't believe I am. I haven't run with the story, which is most likely what they wanted. Expected."

"Maybe not, but you will."

Her mouth tightened, tugging at the edges of her lips and pulling his attention.

"I promise, you're being used. But what concerns me more is that you're deliberately putting yourself in harm's way."

Her head tipped sideways as she studied him. "How am I doing that?"

Was she really that oblivious? Could she really not

see it? No, that wasn't possible. Meredith was one of the most intelligent women he'd ever met.

"These women *have* disappeared. Whatever else is happening, that doesn't usually occur unless there's a reason. And you're standing smack in the middle of it right now."

Meredith's eyes narrowed. Slowly, she closed the gap between them, moving with deliberate grace into his personal space. "That statement tells me you know exactly why they're missing. And where they've gone. Tell me."

She'd maneuvered him. Clever girl.

By his sides, Dominic's hands curled into two tight fists. It was either that or reach for her, pull her in and kiss the hell out of her. And Dominic knew from experience that wouldn't end well.

The heat from her body radiated toward him, touching his skin and making the blood in his veins hum. Her scent drifted across his senses, filling his lungs and invading his body.

She moved closer, murmuring, "You mentioned chaos, but you're standing right in the middle of it next to me."

Unable to resist any longer, he reached out with a hand that was far steadier than he'd expected and brushed the fall of her rich, red hair over the curve of her shoulder. It wasn't enough. Somehow, his fingers found themselves curled around the base of her neck. His thumb stroked the hollow of her throat, absorbing the silky, soft texture of her skin.

"You make it sound like we're allies, backs together as we fight against a common enemy."

"We could be. If you'd let me in." The sincere promise in her eyes was tempting. So tempting. But he knew it wasn't real. Meredith didn't want anything to do with him. And she had no idea what she was offering.

Dominic swallowed against the burn of need ripping through his body. Slowly, he let her go, taking a step backward. "No, we're on opposite sides."

He needed to remember that. Remember why he'd kept his hands to himself for so long where Meredith was concerned. She didn't want him. She didn't like him. And he couldn't be what she needed. What she deserved.

But she didn't take the hint. Instead, she followed him as he tried to back away. "That's where you're wrong, Nic. If what you just said to Annalise is true, we're very much on the same side."

She stalked him. Overwhelmed him. Left him nowhere to hide from what he wanted. Her blue-gray eyes blazed at him. Challenging, demanding.

"It certainly doesn't feel that way," he murmured, right before he thought, *to hell with it*. Grasping her, Dominic pulled her tight against his body. His lips hovered over hers, close enough that the warmth of her breath caressed his mouth.

He waited, giving her a second to pull away if she wanted to. But she didn't. And that was good enough for him.

Closing the minuscule space, his lips found hers. And everything else melted away.

What the hell was she doing kissing him back?

Meredith stood there, his soft shirt bunched into her tight fists as she pulled Dominic closer. Her mouth and hands had a mission of their own, but her mind...it was reeling.

He was doing this on purpose. To distract her. To persuade her.

Dominic had a long history of using sex, charm and his body to get what he wanted. And she'd be damned if she was going to be the next on a long list of women who'd fallen for the tactic.

She was smarter than that.

Finding the strength, Meredith flattened her hands against his chest and pushed.

Dominic took a single step backward, but it was enough. It would have to be enough.

Gasping in air, Meredith reached up to her mouth and swiped the back of her hand across her lips.

"Ouch, angel, now that hurts." His words were silk and seduction, even as they professed to a wound he couldn't feel.

Rocking back onto his heels, he stuffed both hands deep into his pockets and simply grinned down at her.

That smirk only set her more on edge. She'd seen it before and knew it for the lie it was. "Please. We both know nothing I do or say could hurt you. I've known you for a very long time, Dominic, and the only time you've expressed an interest in kissing me was out of pity."

Meredith tried not to let the little cuts from her own words sting. She remembered that night. Vividly. The humiliation she'd felt when he'd kissed her. She'd stood there, watching moonlight pour over his gorgeous face, *wanting* him. Like always.

And if that kiss had been anything besides emotional manipulation, she might have reveled in it. But it hadn't been real. Dominic had felt bad for her. Poor little girl, dumped on the night of the big dance.

She hadn't wanted his pity, so she'd pushed him away.

"You've never once expressed any interest in me. Until now. When you'd like nothing more than to distract me from exposing the truth of whatever's going on."

Dominic took a step forward. Normally, Meredith would have stood her ground, but considering her body was still humming, she thought retreat was a prudent response.

That is, until he matched her step for step and her back hit the cold wall. There was nowhere left to go.

He reached for her again. Meredith turned her head away, hoping to save herself from more temptation. She could have scooted sideways. He wasn't blocking her in. But that was more than she could command of her body right now. Her brain said no, but the rest of her wanted him to touch her. Everywhere.

The pads of his fingers trailed down the exposed

curve of her throat, sending a shiver of unwanted awareness straight down her spine.

"Whatever's going on?" he murmured. "Not what I've been doing. Not the atrocious things you accused me of. Be careful, angel—it's your turn to give yourself away with your words."

Dammit. He was right. Somewhere over the last several hours, between the phone call from Anderson Stone and the interaction between Dominic and Annalise, she'd begun to wonder what the truth truly was.

And begun to believe, whatever it was, Dominic was in trouble.

Leaving her gaze turned away, Meredith responded, "I'm a journalist, looking for the truth. Nothing more. Now, let me go."

Her heart beat against the confining walls of her chest, not from fear, but from proximity. Her body had always reacted to Dominic, even when she didn't want it to. Luckily, keeping her distance had never been much of a problem. Until recently.

She waited, holding her breath, until he finally stepped away. "You've always been free to do just as you like."

Sweeping his hand toward the door, Dominic tipped his head in that direction as he walked away. Taking up his spot beside the wall of windows, he turned, giving her his back and dismissing her.

Meredith wanted to be upset at the gesture. But she was smart enough to realize she needed to leave in order to get herself back under control.

Before she did something she'd seriously regret.

Pushing away from the wall, Meredith headed for the doors. If her legs were less than steady, she took comfort in knowing only she was aware.

The hinges creaked, a blast of noise that sounded much louder to her ears than it probably was. And she was halfway out before his low, smooth voice stopped her.

"Be careful, Meredith. You don't know what you're playing with."

What was she supposed to say to that? They both knew she wasn't going to let this go, so the warning was wasted breath.

But what he said next wasn't.

"And don't fool yourself, angel. I've wanted to touch and taste you for years."

Six

Why had he let that confession slip? No good could come from it. It changed nothing and solved nothing.

But he hadn't been able to stop the words. Some long-buried part of him needed her to know that it hadn't been a calculated move.

Hell, it hadn't been a conscious thought. One minute she was standing in front of him, and the next she was wrapped in his arms.

And she'd felt like the perfection he'd only experienced one other time in his life.

Different than he'd remembered. Better, which surprised him and made him want even more.

Meredith had been all fire in his arms, responding and giving and demanding in a way that lit an answer deep inside him. Even now, the taste of her still swelled through his senses.

For someone who lived her life in such a rigid, exacting manner, she'd absolutely melted for him.

And that experience tempted him. Goaded him. Teased him with what he couldn't have. Because nothing had changed. In fact, everything was worse.

Dominic couldn't touch her again. Meredith deserved so much more than the twisted man that he was. He couldn't be what any woman needed, but definitely not what she deserved.

He'd already proven once in his life that no woman was safe near him. The pain of losing his mother—he never wanted to experience that again.

Meredith, for all her poised, self-righteous attitude, had an unbelievably giving heart. She constantly put the well-being of others before her own. Hell, she'd built an entire career on championing those who couldn't fight for themselves.

She hated him, with good reason. He'd purposely cultivated an identity that flew in the face of everything she stood for. Her low opinion of him had never bothered him before…because it was nothing more than what he thought of himself.

Tonight, it hurt when she pushed away from him. And while the expression on her face hadn't been the horror of his memory, her anger had been close enough.

It was a good thing he planned to avoid her from now on. Hopefully, Stone and Joker were successful in gathering enough support to squash the story.

Preferably before Meredith found herself neck-deep in danger that she couldn't escape.

The door opened behind him, and Dominic had to fight back a growl of frustration. Why couldn't everyone just leave him alone tonight?

Jake didn't wait for him to acknowledge his presence. "We've got a problem."

Of course they did. "What?"

"Someone followed Tessa and me as we left."

"Goddammit."

"That pretty much sums it up. At first, obviously, I was concerned that her husband had somehow tracked her."

With current technology, it was always a concern. They took precautions, but the fear was there. Leaving was potentially the most vulnerable time for any of the women they helped.

Being followed was a definite problem, but one they'd developed contingency plans for.

"I called in backup to follow the tail. When we realized it wasn't Tessa's husband or anyone connected to him, I thought it might be the person who sent the information to Meredith. I decided to use the opportunity to do a little surveillance of my own."

Smart man. There was a reason Jake was the head of his security team. "And...?"

"You're not going to like what I found."

Of course he wasn't. "Just tell me."

"It was a guy, big, tall, muscled."

"Hired?"

"Absolutely, but not by who you'd expect. We trailed him back to a meeting…with Meredith."

He wanted to strangle her. What the hell was she thinking bringing someone else into the situation? Her actions could have cost Tessa her freedom.

"Tessa's still on track?"

"Yes, I contacted Stone and we've changed her itinerary and final destination just to be cautious, but I don't believe she's in any danger."

Well, that was a relief. "This time. That doesn't mean she still couldn't be. Remind the team they need to stay vigilant. These first hours are crucial in her getting away clean."

Jake nodded. "Already done."

And it appeared the promise he'd just made himself to keep his distance from Meredith was going to be short-lived.

It was late. Very late, more morning than night. But Meredith couldn't settle. Her mind simply wouldn't shut off…and her lips kept tingling with a reminder of that kiss.

Holding a glass of wine—her second—she stared out the bedroom window of her condo and hoped the wine would kick in soon so she could get some rest. In the distance, the desert stretched before her, dark, barren and beautifully calm. She much preferred that side of Vegas to the luxury that Annalise embraced or the lights, chaos and excess of Dominic's domain.

Shaking her head, Meredith downed the last of her drink and headed for her en suite. Going through her normal bedtime routine, she slipped into a soft nightie and walked out of her bathroom to stop dead in her tracks.

A man stood on the far side of her bedroom, staring out the same window she'd been peering through not fifteen minutes ago.

Meredith's heart should be racing, and it had definitely taken a quick skip when she'd realized she wasn't alone. But she didn't need to see his face to know who was standing in her bedroom. She'd recognize that wide stance anywhere, the tilt of his head and the way his hands were shoved into his pockets… just as he'd been standing earlier tonight.

The instantaneous hum in her blood was another dead giveaway.

"How the hell did you get in here?"

Dominic turned. His dark, smoky gaze took a leisurely stroll from her naked toes, up her bare thighs and over her silk-clad skin to land finally on her face.

Heat licked through her body, a flame following the trail of his eyes. Her nipples hardened, scraping uncomfortably against soft fabric. Dominic's gaze sharpened, clearly taking in her physical response to his perusal.

Which irritated her even more.

Self-preservation told her she should reach for something and cover up. His silent, steady stare made her feel absolutely naked. But the rest of her realized that he was the invader here, not her, and she could damn well wear whatever she wanted in her own bedroom.

"Expecting company, angel?"

"No."

Dominic hummed in the back of his throat, a non-answer to a question neither of them had really asked. Which reminded her, he'd ignored the question she *had* asked. So she asked it again, "How did you get in here?"

"Let's just say your security measures leave much to be desired."

"For most people, a simple lock and courtesy is enough."

"I'm not most people."

Of that, she was keenly aware. "And by that you mean you believe yourself above common decency and the law? Breaking and entering is a crime, Dominic."

That described him to a T. For Dominic, rules were nothing but suggestions, while for her, they'd dictated her entire life. It went further than that, though. Meredith saw it as injustice when people felt they could play by a different set of rules than everyone else. Hell, she'd built a career out of exposing those kinds of people.

She didn't understand Dominic's ability to simply disregard rules and not care.

He shrugged. "Call the police. But before you do, why don't we have a little chat about the guy you had tailing my head of security?"

Meredith's gaze narrowed. How did he know about that? Ethan wasn't *her* guy, but she really didn't feel the need to point out that tiny defect in his statement. Annalise had offered one of her security team, partly to try and figure out what was going on, but also to add another layer of protection for Dominic.

Because the stubborn man wouldn't ask for help even when he needed it.

Ethan hadn't exactly brought back anything useful. He'd tailed one of Dominic's cars from Excess, but Nic hadn't been inside. One of his employees—clearly the head of security, according to Dominic—and a beautiful woman had been, though. Ethan told her the two had sneaked into a hotel through the back entrance.

"Head of security, huh? It looks like he's being a bit naughty. Using the boss's cars for his own fun?"

Dominic's mouth quirked up. "Oh, he had my permission for everything he was doing."

"I bet."

"You aren't going to let this go, are you?"

Meredith cocked her head to the side and studied Nic for several seconds. Still, so late in the day, he managed to look debonair and polished. Even with his collar undone, his sleeves rolled up and his jacket nowhere in sight.

"Let what go? Your employee's affair?"

"Jake isn't having an affair. I'm talking about the story. No, I'm talking about this whole mess, because clearly your investigator thought he was tailing me. Even if the story gets killed, you won't be able to stop yourself from pulling at the threads to try and solve the puzzle, will you?"

Meredith shrugged. He was right, but something inside her didn't want to admit that. Sure, the story had been the start of it, but now…it was much more.

It was Dominic. And pieces that didn't fit. It was the concern in his eyes when he tried to get her to drop her questions and the certainty in his voice when he said she was going to find herself in danger.

It was the gut-gnawing sensation that something wasn't right. And that Dominic was in trouble.

And she couldn't just walk away.

"Why should I?"

Dominic's mouth twisted into a tight line. "Because I asked you to."

She let out a harsh laugh. "That's hardly a reason for me to do anything, Nic."

Taking several steps closer, Dominic skirted around the huge bed centered in the middle of the room. She'd definitely felt safer with it placed between them. Not because she feared him, but because she feared her own reaction to him.

The need that bubbled just beneath the surface of her skin.

"That's what I assumed you'd say. Your little friend cost me a lot of time and money tonight."

"I hardly see how that's possible." But if he wanted to explain it to her, she was all ears.

Slowly, Dominic closed the gap between them until he was standing inches in front of her. Moonlight filtered across the harsh planes of his face, highlighting his cheekbones and making him look even more dangerous than she already knew he was.

Softly, he murmured, "That's the problem. And I don't owe you an explanation for anything I do."

Meredith's body hummed, with excitement, anticipation and a nervous energy. The lethal cocktail made her skin tingle. She simply wanted him to leave. Before she did something she'd really regret—like take advantage of the bed standing directly behind him.

"I don't remember saying you did," she responded, the words coming out on autopilot while her mind was otherwise occupied by dirty, naughty thoughts.

His lips quirked up into a half smile that somehow managed to hold no humor. "I'm going to give you one anyway, so we can avoid this issue in the future."

Ha! He made it sound like he was doing this out of the goodness of his heart when they both knew very well that whatever Dominic was about to say was more about controlling her than anything else, something he was very good at.

He used that devil-may-care attitude to his advantage and always had. She'd watched him, ever the observer, over the years. The man was intelligent, thorough and highly successful. And yet, people underestimated him. Which was exactly how he liked it.

Whatever he was going to tell her, it wasn't because he'd decided she needed to know. It was because he'd realized it was the only way to get the result he wanted—which was for her to back off.

After he'd tried to intimidate her, stun her with a kiss, sic his influential friend on her and—if the call from one of her editors was an indication—kill her story. He was out of options and left only with finally telling her the truth. Otherwise, he would never be sharing whatever he was about to tell her.

Of that, she was absolutely certain.

Grasping her by the hand, Dominic didn't ask her to follow him, but pulled her across the room to stand at the end of her bed. Hands on her shoulders, he turned her to face the long stretch of mattress and covers. Somewhere deep inside her chest, air stalled in her lungs. The rough pads of his fingers slipped deliciously across her skin.

And with a loud smack, something bounced onto the bed in front of her.

Meredith blinked, her brain taking a moment to catch up to what she was seeing. Open in front of her was a folder filled with documents.

The left side contained a photograph, a familiar face staring up at her.

Turning to take in Dominic behind her, she said, "I don't understand."

His mouth turned into a sad smile. "I know."

"Why do you have a photograph of Tessa?"

She hadn't seen Tessa in months, but she clearly recognized the woman who'd been her friend for years.

"Because she's the woman your investigator saw going into the hotel with Jake tonight."

"What?" Tessa was married and had been for the past six years. "She's having an affair?"

Was Dominic telling her this to distract her? Give her something else to focus on? It wasn't going to work.

Meredith waved her hand, dismissing the entire thing. "I don't care if she is."

Because, honestly, Meredith had never liked Tessa's husband—he'd given her the creeps the few times they'd interacted—so she wasn't entirely upset her friend had found someone better. Even if she didn't approve of Tessa's methods for dealing with that. But she wasn't about to say that to Dominic and sell out her friend.

"She isn't having an affair with Jake."

Okay, now she was really confused. "Then why did they go into that hotel together?"

And how did she really know that had been Tessa? The woman Ethan described looked nothing like her friend, although maybe she'd changed her hair or had been wearing a disguise?

"Because Tessa is disappearing tonight."

Meredith's eyebrows beetled with confusion. It was like he was speaking a foreign language, although she understood every word. "What are you talking about?" Was he admitting Tessa was about to be abducted? Like the other women?

"Tessa's husband is abusive, and as you know, he's a well-respected and connected man within the community."

"Wait, what?" She might not have seen Tessa often over the past few years, but how could she not know her friend was being abused?

"Ben was always careful not to mark her face or leave visible bruises. But a few days ago, he went too far. Cracked four ribs and broke her wrist."

"I'd have known." Wouldn't she? She was an investigative reporter. Trained to see beneath the surface and catch the lies everyone liked to tell to protect their own interests.

"Battered women are often very good at hiding their abuse."

Shaking her head, Meredith still couldn't fit all the pieces together. Reaching out to the file, she started flipping through the pages. Paragraphs and paragraphs of information, including documentation of the abuse that had occurred.

Meredith's stomach rolled as the words swam in front of her. The wine in her belly soured, and she had this sudden urge to take flight. To find Tessa, hold her tight and promise they'd figure this out together.

Snapping the folder closed, Meredith jerked to turn away, to bolt for the door, to do something to help her friend. But the solid wall of Dominic's body stopped her.

Grasping her arms, Nic held her in place. "Don't," he murmured, the single word low and direct.

Meredith fought—against his hold, against the realization of what had been happening to her friend—but she didn't get anywhere. Dominic's strong hands held her tight, making her struggles useless.

Finally, she stopped, letting her body go lax. Not because she was done, but because he'd given her no outlet for the anger coursing through her. She was pissed, and Dominic was the easy target.

Jerking her gaze up, she spit out, "How the hell did you get involved?"

"Tessa's husband is a regular at Excess, sometimes with her, sometimes with a rowdy group of friends. About eight months ago, he was living it up in one of the VIP lounges. Tessa was with him. He was drunk off his ass and surrounded by a group of yes-men who were just as eager to throw their weight around."

Meredith heard the disdain and anger in Dominic's voice. It was a tone she'd never heard from him before. Direct, demanding…passionate. Usually, he always gave the appearance of being completely laidback and uncaring. Now, his eyes, always mesmerizing, roiled with banked irritation.

This was definitely a side of Dominic that was new to her. Any other time, she might have found that intriguing. But she was too tied up in what he was telling her to let herself get sidetracked.

"I watched him verbally abuse and berate Tessa all night. At one point he pulled back his arm, but he probably realized he was in a public place and dropped it without touching her. The way she flinched…" Dominic's jaw tightened, the muscle there ticking.

"Clearly it wasn't the first time. I waited until she went to the restroom and pulled her aside. Reminded her who I was and told her I could get her help. She wasn't ready that night—they usually aren't—but

I gave her a card and told her I could help. She finally called me."

Meredith's stomach turned, but she still had questions. "So, you connected her with a group that could help?"

A smile played at the corner of Dominic's mouth. "In a manner of speaking. I have some very influential friends, and they formulated a plan to help Tessa disappear. She's being provided with a new identity and set up with a new life."

Meredith shook her head. "What? Like witness protection?"

"Sort of."

If that's what was going on with Tessa...

"The women who've disappeared are all victims of domestic violence that you've helped relocate?"

Dominic nodded.

"Why the hell didn't you just say that?"

"Because every person who knows is a potential danger to those women. In every case, they're hiding from very powerful, influential men. There's a reason they run instead of reporting the abuse. Police officers, federal law enforcement, businessmen, judges, billionaires and high rollers. Men with reach and resources."

Seven

Dominic watched Meredith's reaction. He could see thoughts whirling inside her brain as she connected the dots.

And it was the strangest thing, to have a firsthand view as her entire opinion of him shifted.

Meredith had never particularly liked him.

She'd never bothered to hide the fact that she found his lifestyle objectionable. She didn't like the way he treated women—never caring to understand that the women he engaged with were perfectly fine with the arrangement. She felt his business contributed nothing beneficial to society and had often gotten on his case about doing something valuable. Contributing in some way.

She saw him as nothing more than a man who

profited from excess and enjoyed living the same party lifestyle that he promoted.

Her opinion of him wasn't important. Or, he'd always told himself that was true. He'd never felt the need to correct her. To point out that Excess Inc. contributed millions of dollars to various worldwide charities. Or tell her the stories of employees that he'd personally assisted with college tuition, medical care or other expenses when they'd encountered life's difficult moments. Not to mention the people he employed, the generous benefits he provided or the stringent security measures he put in place to protect the patrons who were incapacitated enough that they couldn't protect themselves.

She wanted to see him as a charming playboy, caring for nothing but his own pleasure, and he'd never dissuaded her.

Because he liked the barrier between them. It kept him from pining for things he couldn't have. It was easier and kept his own unacknowledged desire for her chained up so he didn't have to confront it. It kept him from convincing himself that he could take a risk and try.

Meredith stared at him for several seconds, her bright blue eyes calculating. "You protect abused women and provide them with new identities," she finally said.

It wasn't a question, but he answered it, anyway. "Yes."

"That must be expensive."

"It is."

"You pay for that?"

He wanted to tell her no. To knock some of the surprised admiration out of her gaze and put back just an inkling of the disdain that usually lurked there when she saw him.

That was smarter. Safer.

But he couldn't lie to her. "Not all of it."

"But some of it."

Dominic shrugged. "There are several of us involved."

"Anderson Stone."

Stone wasn't going to appreciate having his involvement revealed, especially to a reporter. Dominic would deal with the consequences later. "Yes, Stone Surveillance is involved."

He expected her to ask questions about how the operation worked. What role did each of them play? Where were the women—something he'd never reveal, not even to her.

Instead, she asked a completely unexpected question. And because he hadn't braced for it, his mouth answered before his brain could stop him.

"Why? Why do you get involved?"

The truth was simple. "Because no one protected my mother, and my life would have been completely different if someone had."

The night his mother had died at the hands of her husband, his stepfather, was the worst experience of his life. But he never talked about it, and he didn't want to start now.

But Meredith, being Meredith, was no doubt about

to pepper him with all sorts of questions. Because she simply couldn't let anything go.

Gritting his teeth, Dominic prepared for the on-slaught, ready to shut her down. But no questions came. Instead, Meredith tipped her head sideways and after several seconds slowly closed the gap be-tween them.

She didn't touch him, but she was close enough that the heat from her body did. And the scent of her, the natural musk and vanilla combined with a hint of floral from whatever lotion she'd rubbed into her skin before slipping that scrap of a nightie over her body, reached out for him instead.

"I never asked Annalise, but I knew whatever hap-pened that night wasn't good. And the story every-one told wasn't true."

Of course she'd known. Because she was smart and could see the holes from a mile away. But his stepfather was powerful, just like the men who'd hurt the women he rescued. And it had been his and An-nalise's word against their stepfather's.

The two of them had been young, ten and eight. Scared and in shock. By the time the officers—who were no doubt in his stepfather's pockets—had got-ten finished with their interviews, they'd confused both children enough that their stories were a jum-bled mess that they could then say were unreliable.

Their account was explained away as two fright-ened children who weren't entirely certain what had transpired that night but were trying to protect the memory of their mentally ill mother by placing blame somewhere else.

So he'd gotten away with it.

Dominic didn't see the reason in confirming her statement, though, so he silently watched her, his hands itching to reach for her and close the minuscule gap that was now between them.

He wanted to taste her mouth again. To run his hands across the silky texture of her skin. To rip that tantalizing lace right off her body and explore every inch of her. To hear her scream his name and beg for more.

He wanted what he'd never given himself permission to take.

"Your mother wasn't crazy. She didn't attack your stepfather. It wasn't an accident."

Slowly, Dominic shook his head. Hearing the words—the truth—after all these years, from someone who actually believed them, was…a relief. In a way that he hadn't understood he needed until Meredith said them.

"And you're honoring her memory by helping others like her."

Dominic swallowed the rough lump in the back of his throat. Yes, clearly that's what he was doing. He'd always known that, but no one else had. Not even Gray or Stone. They'd never questioned why he was willing to spend his money, use his business and put his reputation in jeopardy to help total strangers. Possibly because they did the same thing.

But it was nice for someone to recognize and understand.

Closing the last several inches, Meredith pushed into his personal space. The heavy weight of her palm landed in the center of his chest, and she rolled up on her toes, murmuring, "I see you, Nic. Finally," before pressing her mouth to his.

Meredith couldn't stop the impulse to kiss him anymore than she could stop herself from breathing. Oh, she could have tried, but it would have been pointless. Eventually, her body would have taken over anyway and claimed what she needed to survive.

And right now, the deep-seated need she'd ignored for years was finally demanding to be freed.

Maybe it was the expression in Dominic's eyes, a little lost, a lot sad and so devastated, that made her do it. Something hard in the center of her chest squeezed. And all she could think about was giving him something else—something better—to think about instead of the painful past that clearly haunted him.

It had been so much easier to keep her desire for him banked behind self-righteous judgment and cold indignation. But once he'd ripped those away…his pain echoed through her own chest, and she wanted to make it disappear.

The kiss started out soft, soothing. A gentle gift and a subtle exploration.

But it didn't stay that way.

At first, Dominic took what she was giving. He drank it in and let her take the lead. But it wasn't long before his hands were fisted into her hair, tugging her head backward so that he could get more.

His tongue thrust deep into her mouth, teasing, exploring, sending bolts of need straight through her belly to settle at her core. Pinpricks of excitement scattered across her scalp where he pulled.

Slowly, he urged her backward until the backs of her knees hit the edge of the bed. But she didn't fall. She wasn't ready. She still wanted more.

Dominic released her mouth, and Meredith pulled a huge gulp of air deep into her lungs. The room spun a little, from lack of oxygen or being physically off-kilter? It didn't matter—she reached for that minute reprieve, hoping it would help her get her body back under control.

But the moment was too short to be helpful. Not when his mouth almost immediately found purchase at the side of her neck. The burning heat of his lips trailed across her skin, leaving a path of devastating need behind.

Her skin tingled and burned. He reached the tiny pulse buried at the side of her throat and sucked. A strangled sound escaped Meredith's parted lips. An answering growl rumbled through Dominic's chest. Her palms splayed wide across his torso; she felt the sound just as much as heard it. Experienced the echo of it deep inside.

He was driving her crazy and he'd barely done more than hold her and kiss her. Her core throbbed with an endless need that only he could relieve. Was it possible to orgasm just from his mouth on her skin?

Meredith shook her head, mentally calling herself ten kinds of stupid, and not just for the way her body was reacting. It was one thing to recognize he had more integrity than he'd ever let on.

But his reputation with women wasn't fabricated. It was real. Dominic didn't do relationships. From the time they were teenagers, he'd always been the same. Flatter and charm until they fell at his feet. She'd never wanted to be one of those women, who was stupid enough to think he would be different for them. Because he never was, and that was just asking for heartache.

Meredith had never bothered to ask him why. It didn't really matter why. Tonight, everything felt different. *He* felt different. His need for her was clear and real. Overwhelming and thrilling.

Could she be okay with taking what she wanted now and not worrying about what came after?

In the middle of the building storm, Dominic suddenly pulled back. Slipping his fingers beneath the tiny line of strap that trailed her shoulder, the backs of his fingers brushed against Meredith's skin.

He stared into her. The intensity in his eyes…too much. That dark, steady gaze devoured her. He *saw* her. Saw everything. And for a split second she wondered if he always had.

Meredith had never felt so naked in her entire life. Utterly exposed in a way that was both exhilarating and frightening.

"Tell me to stop." The dark, rich rumble of his voice was one more caress to her already overloaded senses. Like hot caramel melting cold ice cream, her own residual inhibitions just disappeared.

"No" was her only answer. She wouldn't tell him to stop. She didn't want him to stop.

The sound of ripping threads was his only response as his looped fingers snapped the flimsy material holding up one side of her nightie. Meredith let out a gasp. Not because she particularly cared about the ruined piece of lingerie, but because the sudden gust of cold air across her sensitive nipple was a shock.

More so than Dominic tearing her clothes off.

She'd always known he'd be a physical and demanding lover. And she hadn't needed to hear the legendary stories that had swirled around him to know that would be the case.

She might not agree with the persona Dominic wore like a mask, but part of that was because she'd always known deep down he was better than the not-a-care-in-the-world act. God, it pissed her off that he was wasting his true intensity and dedication.

Well, she was the recipient of it all right now. And while it was overwhelming, it was also exhilarating. Dominic made her feel…powerful. Wanted. Sexy. And she was going to take advantage of it while she could.

Free of its bindings on one side, the silky fabric slithered down her body, pooling at her waist and leaving one breast totally bare.

Dominic didn't waste any time in taking advantage. Dipping his head, he sucked her distended nipple deep into his mouth and tugged. Delicious sensations spiraled through her. Dropping her head back, Meredith closed her eyes and simply fell into the experience.

Both hands cupped his head as she urged him to give her more. Scraping the edge of his teeth softly against her skin, Dominic pulled back until the tight bud of her nipple was held captive. With teasing flicks, he ran his tongue over the knot of flesh.

Meredith squirmed beneath the onslaught. It felt so good. But it wasn't nearly enough.

Reaching up, she pushed the other strap off her shoulder. The nightie slipped down her body, pooling at her feet.

Dominic let go just long enough to take her in.

God, she was gorgeous. The bright hair she normally kept in a tail or a twist floated down around her shoulders, free. He loved it this way and always had. It made her look more carefree, less single-minded and focused.

Human, with desires, needs, hopes and fears. It made him feel that maybe, just maybe he wouldn't sully her completely by touching her.

Not that it would matter right now if he did. He was too far gone. He'd given her the chance to walk away, and when she'd said no…he didn't have the strength to deny them anymore.

Moonlight spilled through the windows to gild her

olive skin. And her eyes, the most gorgeous blue gray he'd ever seen, burned with a fire he felt deep inside.

"You're gorgeous."

Meredith tipped her head sideways. She didn't attempt to cover her body or hide from him. She didn't try to play the coy seductress. Confident in her own skin, feet spread wide, she simply let him look.

But as much as he was enjoying taking in the beauty of her body, he wasn't content to simply gaze at her. He wanted to devour, to taste and touch.

With a flick of her hand, Meredith silently demanded that he take his own clothes off. As much as he'd have loved her hands on him, removing each piece, it was just as sexy that she wanted to watch.

Without breaking the contact of her stare, Dominic slowly pushed each of the buttons down the center of his shirt through their tiny holes before tossing it onto a chair. His belt was next, the only sounds in the room that of the clanging metal and the harsh in and out of Meredith's breaths.

Slowly, he pushed his slacks and shorts over his hips, and, toeing off the loafers he'd slipped on this morning, left everything else in a pile at his feet.

Stepping over it all, he left his clothes behind him. But he didn't reach for her. Instead, he spread his own feet wide and let her feast on him with those fire-and-ice eyes.

Color glowed across her skin as she perused his body, taking her sweet time to linger on the expanse of his shoulders, the V at the bottom of his abs and finally the jutting length of his sex. The sharp, pink tip of her tongue darted out across her lips, leaving a shiny trail that he wanted to follow with his own.

But he waited for some reaction. Never in his life had he been nervous standing naked in front of a woman. Dominic was confident and charming. He'd been pleasing women for years. He knew what they liked and, more importantly, what they needed. But Meredith…her opinion of him mattered.

More than it should.

Finally, she said, "I'd give you a compliment, but it wouldn't be anything you haven't heard a hundred times. You're beautiful, and you know it."

Unexpected laughter erupted up through Dominic's chest. "That might be true, but I wouldn't mind hearing it from you. Compliments are easy and unimportant… unless they come from someone you respect."

"You don't respect me."

That had him surging forward. Grasping her hair in his hands, he relished the soft, velvety texture even as he used it to bend her backward, forcing her to lock eyes with him.

"That's bullshit, and you know it. I respect the hell out of you. Why do you think I've kept my hands to myself all these years? Sex is easy, angel. There's nothing about you that's easy. You're the definition of complicated."

Eight

Warm heat chased through her, settling deep in her belly. It wasn't just a physical response, but something more. Something akin to the happy, comforting feeling that homemade chocolate chip cookies can give you when they're baked with love.

What the hell was she supposed to do with that?

Right now, Meredith was desperately trying to hang on to reality. To not let herself get wrapped up in Dominic. In this. To simply enjoy it for what it was—a sexual encounter that would no doubt blow her mind.

But if he kept saying things like that...

"Well, let's uncomplicate things, then. I'm fully aware of your mantra, Nic. And I'm happy to live by your rules."

Dominic's mouth pulled tight. "And what do you think those are?"

Meredith shrugged, trying not only to adopt the appearance of being unconcerned but to convince herself it was true. "Like you said, sex is easy. We clearly both want each other. And it doesn't need to go any further than that. Let's enjoy tonight and go back to normal tomorrow."

Normal being Meredith would avoid him as much as possible.

Dominic's reaction surprised her. She would have expected him to immediately agree…it was what he did, after all. But instead, his eyes narrowed. His fingers, already tangled through her hair, tightened, tugging deliciously at her scalp. His other arm wrapped around her waist, holding her close and supporting her weight.

Meredith felt caught and cared for at the same time. An unfamiliar and uncomfortable sensation. Why wouldn't he just go back to kissing her?

The long, hard evidence of Dominic's desire for her pressed against her hip. He wanted her. And she wanted him. Couldn't that be enough?

With a sudden burst of movement, he swept her up into his arms and urged her backward. Meredith found herself stretched across the bed. The rough texture of her duvet scratched against her naked skin, and the unexpected change in location sent her head spinning…again.

Dominic's wicked mouth glided across her body.

Sucking pulse points. Laving nipples. Leaving tiny marks that tingled and burned.

It didn't take long before Dominic had Meredith writhing beneath him. She silently searched for relief from the burning need he created. Something, anything that would alleviate the ache. But all she found was him.

Her hands grasped mindlessly for pieces of him she could take just as surely as he was demanding pieces of her. His half groan, half moan of need when she finally wrapped her palm around the hard length of him and stroked was pure magic.

That sound made her feel powerful, provocative. Sexy as hell because she'd coaxed that involuntary noise from him.

Using her strength, and the element of surprise, Meredith reared up and pushed at Dominic's shoulders until he dropped onto the bed beside her. His back to the mattress, she quickly straddled him.

Astride his hips, she pressed the throbbing core of her sex against the hard ridge of his and rolled her body. Relief, that's what she needed. Demanded. The delicious sensation had her head dropping back in bliss.

But it still wasn't enough.

Leaning sideways, Meredith yanked at the drawer in the bedside table and fished around for several seconds before finding what she wanted. Dropping back onto her thighs, she held up a flat foil square in triumph.

With a soft chuckle, Dominic snapped the condom

out of her fingers and said, "I should have known you'd always be prepared."

She shrugged. It paid for a woman to look out for herself. Meredith didn't bother to wait for him to do the job. Using her leverage, she snatched the packet back, tore it open and had the condom rolled down over his beautiful cock almost before he could blink.

Okay, so maybe she enjoyed his sharp hiss and the way his hips bucked beneath hers as she'd smoothed the circle of latex over him just a little. But her enjoyment was short-lived, because he took advantage of her distraction by flipping her onto her back once again.

A power struggle. Even in bed, that's what it always came down to with him. With them. But tonight, Meredith was willing to give. Because she had no doubt she'd receive more than enough in return.

Hooking an arm under her knee, Dominic spread her hips wide, but instead of thrusting deep inside her, he used his other hand to run his fingers up the inside of her exposed thigh. He teased at the entrance to her sex, rolling his thumb over the tight bundle of nerves pulsing rhythmically to the beat of her speeding heart.

He had her pinned, motionless, right where he wanted. The long length of him poised so close as he teased and tortured her with those delicious fingers and the tantalizing presence of relief just out of her grasp.

She wanted to feel him deep inside, but apparently he had other ideas. It was all too much, and the tension he was expertly building finally exploded.

The orgasm slammed into Meredith. She arched back, her hips thrusting forward, searching, chasing each sensation as the world around her narrowed to the epicenter of pleasure he created.

And then there was more. Meredith didn't even have a chance to gather her breath before he gave her what she'd wanted all along. He thrust deep, his hips colliding with hers. His arm still hooked beneath her knee, Dominic held her captive as he moved in and out. Slow and steady at first, the pace grew until they were both racing.

Panting, their breaths mingled. His mouth found patches of her naked skin—neck, chest, shoulder—and sucked. The world grayed even as moonlight slashed across his glorious body, making him glow. Oh, but Dominic Mercado was far from celestial, even if he could make her body sing like the angels.

Together, they stretched for that beautiful moment of relief.

The second orgasm hit her like an avalanche, blocking out everything except Dominic and how he could make her feel. He threw his own head back in ecstasy, and Meredith felt the rhythmic throb of his release deep inside.

In those moments, she thought he might be the most glorious sight she'd ever seen. But maybe that was just the sex talking.

Together, they collapsed onto the bed, a tangle of arms and legs, racing hearts and sweat-slicked skin.

His weight should have been suffocating, but right now Meredith felt utterly perfect, and she definitely didn't want him to move. Yet.

But it wasn't long before reality and exhaustion stole that glow. Her mind began to whirl with the implications of what they'd just done.

Restlessness had her wiggling, and Dominic responded by rolling them both and tucking her into the crook of his body. Her back to his chest, the pressure inside eased. The moist heat of his breath tickled across her neck. It should have bothered her, but for some reason it didn't.

And in that moment, she was too tired to wonder why. Utter exhaustion stole through her body. Her sluggish mind had enough power to think that if she wasn't careful, she could get used to falling asleep wrapped in the heat of Dominic's body.

Without really thinking about it, she murmured, "Stay," before dropping into a deep sleep.

But when she woke, she was absolutely alone.

Dominic didn't particularly care about spending the night with a woman. It didn't matter one way or the other whether they woke up sharing a bed—the result was the same. He never spent more than a few days with any one woman. They enjoyed each other for as long as it lasted and then both went their separate ways.

Which raised the question—why hadn't he been able to settle with Meredith beside him?

She'd easily dropped into a solid sleep, burrowing

into the covers and his own body like she was seeking any source of warmth. He, on the other hand, couldn't get comfortable. Which was unusual.

Dominic's mind had raced as he watched her sleep. Awake, she was forceful, demanding and judgmental. Asleep, she was soft and appeared fragile, even if he knew she wasn't.

The idea of waking up next to her…felt right.

Which was why he'd left.

He couldn't have *right*. He couldn't risk *right*. Especially with Meredith.

Grabbing his clothes, Dominic slipped into her den and dressed quietly before walking out the front door. He made sure to twist the lock before leaving, not just to keep her safe, but to prevent himself from going back inside. Not that a lock would stop him if he really wanted back in.

It was more of a gesture. A reminder.

She'd said so herself—before they'd devoured each other like they were starving—this was a one-time thing. Undeniable energy sizzled between them, and they'd simply given in. Physical response. Chemistry and biology. Nothing more.

Hell, she didn't even like him. And while that had never been a requirement for him before with a woman, Dominic realized with Meredith he wanted it to be.

Her opinion of him mattered, dammit. Even when it shouldn't.

Dropping into the seat of his Maserati, Dominic let his head fall back against the supple leather.

Closing his eyes, he pulled in a deep breath before letting it out again.

He wouldn't see her again, at least not for a while. He and Meredith had been good at avoiding each other over the years, and there was no reason that shouldn't continue now. He'd effectively convinced her to drop the story, which should move her out of harm's way.

The spurt of relief that thought brought was short-lived. Because while she was safe, he definitely wasn't.

It had been several days since Meredith had woken up alone in her bed. Days when she'd had to work hard not to think about Dominic or the amazing sex they'd shared.

It irritated her that he was so difficult to forget. She'd find herself staring off into space, remembering, at the most inopportune times.

Really, part of her hated that she now understood why all those women had thrown themselves at his feet. He was gorgeous, charismatic, sexy and, damn him, stellar in bed.

Not to mention, he did have a heart after all.

Maybe if she'd been able to talk to her best friend about the encounter, she could have purged the experience instead of letting it marinate in her brain. Instead, she'd spent hours during the day actively keeping herself busy so that she wouldn't remember. But at night, no such luck. Several times she'd woken up, aching and restless from steamy dreams featuring Dominic front and center.

"What the heck is wrong with you?"

And Annalise was clearly starting to notice.

"You aren't still chewing on the Dominic thing, are you?"

Horror and adrenaline flooded Meredith's system. How the hell had Annalise found out?

But her friend continued, sending relief coursing behind it. "I know you never submitted the story, so I assumed something you found convinced you to let it go."

Meredith had never mentioned it again. She couldn't explain why she'd dropped the story without revealing Dominic's secret…or that they'd had sex before he'd sneaked away from her in the middle of the night like a thief.

Really, that was what pissed her off. She couldn't decide if he was being a first-class prick or if he was being a coward. Although, since she'd never known Nic to be a coward, she was leaning toward prick.

He'd swayed her with the revelation that he was capable of good deeds. Apparently, she should have listened to her gut and gone with the impression she'd always had of him. Dominic was self-centered and egotistical, end of story.

Annalise was staring at her. Meredith realized she'd been silent too long and needed to respond. "Yeah, I dropped the story. You were convinced it wasn't true before I was, which is why I didn't mention it."

Hopefully her friend would buy the excuse. They were supposed to be enjoying a nice brunch on the patio outside Annalise's apartment on the penthouse floor of the casino. Living and working in a place with free room service definitely had its perks.

An array of meats, cheeses, crackers and tiny toast squares spread out before them. Rich berries and the most decadent display of bite-size tarts, cakes and chocolates provided dessert. The food at Magnifique was five-star, right along with the breathtaking view.

While it wasn't normally her cup of tea, Meredith had to admit the hustle and bustle of the Strip laid out below them was a bit of a distraction. Or should have been.

The sunshine was definitely nice, especially with the cool breeze wafting through the covered space. Picking up her flute filled with a cranberry mimosa, Meredith took a sip and realized she needed to catch up. Annalise was already on her second glass.

"I still can't believe Tessa is missing. I know it's been a long time since we spoke to her, but she was a friend, and it's so scary to think about what she's going through."

Two days after her night with Dominic, the news that Tessa had gone missing hit the media. Guilt twisted through Meredith's belly. Guilt over Tessa. And guilt for keeping the truth from Annalise.

But she'd promised Dominic she wouldn't tell anyone else about the truth. And even if he didn't deserve her loyalty, she didn't break promises. Besides, she knew Dominic had good reasons for why he didn't want Annalise knowing the truth.

And despite everything, someone clearly wanted to make Dominic's life difficult. Or destroy his life and get him accused of some very serious crimes. He wouldn't want Annalise caught up in that.

Taking a deep breath, Meredith steeled her resolve. She needed to make it through the next few days. Eventually everyone would move on, and Tessa's disappearance would be forgotten. Which both saddened her and gave her a weird sense of hope.

Tessa deserved to find happiness, and if she needed to disappear to do it…

She murmured her agreement before leaning forward. "I don't know about you, but I can't resist another one of those lemon tarts," she said, stuffing one in her mouth. When in doubt, misdirection usually worked.

They were lounging on Annalise's balcony, soaking up the sunshine, when the whoosh of the French doors signaled someone walking out onto the wide concrete space. Meredith's back was to the door, but judging by Annalise's huge smile, she was happy to see whoever had joined them.

A mirrored smile on her face, Meredith turned to investigate, but that smile crashed when she realized Dominic was their visitor.

And instead of making a path toward his sister, his gaze zeroed straight in on her.

"We need to talk."

Shaking her head, Meredith said, "What could we possibly have to talk about?"

Okay, so her words were a little testy. If she wasn't careful, he'd figure out just how irritated she was by his disappearing act.

Tilting his head to the side, Dominic didn't answer with words, but indicated with his pointed expression that whatever he wanted to say shouldn't involve his sister.

Which was his problem, considering he'd tracked her down to Annalise's apartment. Which raised the question... "How did you know I was here?"

"Annalise mentioned you were having a girls' day."

Meredith swung a questioning gaze across to her friend. Annalise just shrugged. "What? I didn't think it was a secret."

The knowing, glowing expression in Annalise's gaze as she looked back and forth between the two of them made Meredith's stomach knot and twist. Great. Somehow, her friend had figured it out. "What gave it away?"

"You mean other than the sparks striking off you two whenever you're in the same room?"

"Right," Meredith grumbled. "We don't strike sparks."

"Please, there's enough energy arcing between you that I have to be careful with the amount of product I put in my hair when you're both around. I'm afraid it'll burst into flames."

Pushing up from the lounge chair, Annalise apparently decided to give them space. Crossing the balcony, she headed for the French doors. Brushing past her brother, she leaned in and gave him a soft kiss on the cheek before disappearing inside.

Meredith stood to follow. Maybe she didn't want to hear what Dominic had to say. But she didn't get very far. He snagged her arm as she tried to pass by and pulled her to a halt.

She stood beside him, refusing to give him what he wanted by turning in his direction. But also unable to simply walk away. The feel of his hand sliding across her bare arm had energy prickling beneath her skin.

"We need to talk."

"You said that already." It irritated her that he thought he could simply reappear, crook his finger and she would jump to do what he wanted. "I've dropped the article. You made it clear you didn't want or need anything else from me when you skulked away in the middle of the night. What could we possibly have to discuss?"

His fingers on her arm tightened. Flexing his hold, he pulled her closer against his body. "Don't be catty, Meredith. It doesn't suit you."

Meredith's gaze finally met his. "Catty? Me? Never," she said, a confrontational grin curling her lips.

His eyes smoldered, dark, swirling green. They reminded her of the forest right before dusk, deep with shadows and dangerous things. Dangerous. That's what he was.

Her belly rolled, not from fear, but from unwanted anticipation. From need.

Now that she'd experienced the power they created, the intensity when he let go, she wanted more.

But he'd made it clear that wasn't going to happen. And she refused to beg.

Dominic huffed and slowly, the darkness in his gaze melted away. His grip on her arm eased, but instead of letting her go, he leaned closer. "Look, I'm sorry I left without saying goodbye."

"Not necessary. We both got what we wanted."

"Hardly," he murmured, the single word so low that she almost missed it.

But since she'd heard it, she'd be damned if she'd let it go. "Excuse me? We both know you damn well got off. Spectacularly, I might add. So don't try and give me that shit."

Closing his eyes, Dominic pulled in a deep breath. Twisting, he tugged her around the bend of the slick stone wall, pressing her back against the smooth surface. From this vantage point they were hidden from Annalise's view inside the penthouse.

Dominic crowded her personal space. Meredith had nowhere to go. She was caught between the solid wall of his body and the stone at her back. But, God help her, she didn't want to be anywhere else.

Which irritated the hell out of her. When had she lost control of her own body? Her pulse jumped. Her heart knocked repeatedly against her ribs. And her sex throbbed with the memory of the pleasure he could give her. With nothing more than the press of his body against hers, her panties were damp with need for him.

Damn him straight to hell.

She refused to simply stand here, defenseless while he bent her to his will. Folding her arms in front of her, Meredith tried to put a barrier between them. Not that it helped much. She could still feel the heat of him. Sense the solid presence of his body, and hers—traitor that it was—physically responded.

"That's not what I meant," he growled. "I left because we both know this can never work. We're too different. Hell, you don't particularly like me."

Meredith opened her mouth to argue with him but then slammed it shut. Maybe she'd told herself she didn't particularly like him. She'd definitely told him that often enough.

But what if it wasn't true?

"I wanted to be there, Meredith, which was exactly why I left. We both enjoyed the other night. And I wanted to keep those memories. You, sexy, rumpled and sleepy beside me. Hot as hell in my arms. Rather than some awkward morning after that would wipe away what we shared."

Jesus, how could he both make her blood sing and make her want to take a verbal chunk out of him at the same time? With one single breath, he made her feel like she was standing on top of the world, and then he pulled her right down into the muck.

She'd been upset when she woke alone because some secret part of her had wanted more. And she'd been pissed because he'd taken that away from them both.

But, really, wasn't he right?

With a sigh, Meredith dropped her arms. Her head fell back against the wall. Bastard had taken her angry away, which left her with nothing except the wanting. But that was her problem, not his.

"Fine. I'm not mad at you for leaving."

"Bullshit, but if it's any consolation, I'm upset with myself for that." Reaching up, he snagged a strand of her hair and ran the pads of his fingers down the full length. "I was more irritated that I wanted to stay, though."

Damn him.

Shaking her head, Meredith pulled the hair from his grasp. She really didn't need the tingles across her scalp, not when he was listing all the reasons they couldn't work.

"So, if it wasn't to talk about the other night, why did you track me down?"

Taking a step backward, Dominic thrust clenched fists into his pockets and rolled up onto the balls of his feet.

Meredith was starting to realize that was the stance he took when he was confronting something he wasn't excited about tackling.

"I wanted to ask who you told about Tessa's disappearance."

"No one."

"Not even Annalise?"

Meredith frowned. "You asked me not to. I might not agree with you, but I wouldn't go behind your back and tell her without talking to you first."

The ghost of a smile touched his lips. "I appreciate that."

Dominic started to turn away, but it was Meredith's turn to reach out and stop him. "Explain why you just asked me that."

His lips pulled into a hard line, and the concern swimming through his eyes tied a knot deep inside her belly.

"Tessa's missed her scheduled check-ins the last three days."

Nine

Dominic's words hung in the air. He watched as Meredith's mind spun on the information, but he didn't have time to wait for her to process.

Stepping sideways, he tried to move past her, but her body shifted to stop him.

"Where are you going?"

He thought that was fairly obvious, but… "I'm leaving."

"Oh, no, you're not. You can't just track me down, drop this bombshell and then walk away."

A tight smile tugged at his lips. "Watch me."

"Dominic, seriously, did you really expect me just to shrug my shoulders and say okay after telling me my friend is missing and possibly in danger?"

Honestly, he hadn't thought that far ahead. The

first time Tessa had missed her check-in, he'd been concerned but not panicked. The second time…his only thought had been that they'd never had a problem before Meredith had learned the truth. And while she'd dropped the story, that didn't necessarily mean she'd kept the information to herself.

He trusted his team and Stone Surveillance. Meredith…she was untested. So he'd been fairly certain any potential leak would have come from her.

But he believed her when she said she hadn't told anyone. Which meant there was something else going on, and he needed to figure out what. Right now. Tessa had already been missing for three days.

He never should have waited.

Shaking off Meredith's hold, Dominic said, "This isn't any concern of yours."

"The hell you say. She's my friend."

"Was your friend, and I'm going to guess you haven't been close in a very long time."

The guilt that crossed Meredith's face made him feel like the ass he was. He'd said the words on purpose, but getting the reaction he'd been looking for hardly made him feel good.

Son of a bitch.

"I'm sorry. I shouldn't have said that. Whatever's going on isn't your fault."

"Maybe." The tone in her voice suggested she didn't believe him, but Dominic didn't have time to convince her right now. "What are you going to do?"

With a shrug, he said, "Find her." It was that simple. No matter what it took, he'd promised Tessa she'd be safe, and he intended to keep that promise.

"How?"

"I'm going to hop on a plane and see if I can figure out where she's gone and why she's missing. We already have surveillance on her husband, so we know he didn't follow her."

But that hardly meant she was safe. Ben had enough resources and the brains to realize that he potentially needed an alibi if anything happened to Tessa. He could have easily hired someone to track down his recalcitrant wife.

"I'm coming with you."

Her words shouldn't have surprised him, but they did. Not only that, but the idea of Meredith going with him had tension twisting through his gut. "The hell you are."

Meredith's gaze narrowed. "Can you afford to turn down another set of eyes and ears? Especially an investigative reporter adept at studying puzzles and putting the pieces together?"

Dominic's lips pursed. She had a point. A good one. He stared at her for several seconds. Was he telling her no because he didn't want to deal with her or the residual energy and attraction that was far from sated after their one night together?

If that was the case, wasn't he being the coward he'd assured her that he wasn't? And denying her help would be denying Tessa help, something he really couldn't afford to do.

"Fine," he finally said, unable to control the grimace that accompanied the single word.

"Don't look so excited about it."

"Trust me, I won't. I'm leaving in an hour. Pack a bag and meet me at Excess in forty-five minutes. If you're not there, I'm leaving without you."

Dominic turned to go and wasn't altogether surprised when Meredith followed him.

Annalise, lounging on the bar stool at her kitchen island, sipping on a mimosa, grinned at him. "Do I want to know what you were doing behind that wall?"

His sister's cat-eating-the-canary satisfaction made Dominic's tension ratchet higher. The last thing he needed was Annalise getting crazy ideas about him with her best friend.

He decided the best way to handle her was to ignore the question. Stopping long enough to buss her cheek, he said, "See you, sunshine," before walking out the front door.

Behind him, he could still hear his sister. "Wait, you're leaving, too?"

And Meredith's response, "Yeah, I'll be gone for a couple days. Would you water my plants and keep an eye on my place?"

Great, it wasn't going to take a genius—which his sister was—to figure out wherever Meredith was going, it had something to do with him.

Luckily, the elevator arrived before Meredith did. Because right now, he didn't have the strength to deal with her or his sister. Maybe, if he was lucky, an hour would give him enough time to regain control of his emotions.

Control was exactly what he needed. He'd learned long ago that in order to protect the people around him, he had to maintain a tight rein on his own emotions and responses. That lesson had come at a high price.

Right now, Meredith was excelling at breaking through that resolve, which was something he really needed to fix.

Forty-five minutes was cutting it damn close. And he knew it. Meredith had no doubt Dominic would leave without her if she was even a single second late.

Honestly, she half expected to find him already gone when she arrived at Excess. It hadn't occurred to her until he'd left that Dominic could simply be telling her that he was fine with her coming so that she'd leave him alone without a fuss.

However, when she walked into the main offices, it was clear Dominic was still there. She could hear his voice, raised as he bellowed down the hallway at one of his employees.

"Don't forget to double-check the Jack Daniel's order."

Meredith watched as a petite blonde rolled her eyes. "I've got it, Nic. Trust me, I can handle my job."

Dominic slid into the open doorway. Both hands braced on the jamb, a frown pulled at the edges of his mouth. "I know you can. If you couldn't you wouldn't still be here."

Turning her back on him, the blonde marched down the hall muttering under her breath, "What bug crawled up his ass?"

Several others bustled around, shuffling papers and answering phones. A far cry from the quiet, muted feel of the office she'd visited several nights ago, today the Excess executive offices bustled with activity.

From the opposite end of the hallway, Dominic said, "You're here."

He didn't bother to try and hide the disappointment in his voice. Whatever. He could not like it all he wanted, but that wasn't going to change anything.

Striding past the other offices, Meredith tried to ignore the curious looks from everyone she passed. None of their business why she was visiting the boss and carrying an overnight bag.

Dominic didn't move as she approached. He stood in the doorway, arms outstretched, blocking her path into his domain. She didn't bother telling him to move. From the set expression on his sharp features, he wouldn't have done it, anyway.

"Of course I'm here. But you didn't tell me where we're going, so I had to guess on wardrobe."

"I'm sure you'll be fine. And if you're not, you can buy whatever you need."

Sure, like she could just pick up an entire new wardrobe. He might be loaded—and from circulated rumors, that number was close to a billion—but she wasn't. She didn't correct him, though. What was the point? He'd simply use it as an excuse for her not to go.

And that wasn't an option.

If Tessa was in trouble, this time she was going to be there to help. But it would be nice to know their destination. And, really, was that asking too much? "You're not going to tell me, are you?"

His lips—the same ones she'd been trying to forget the last several days—curled up into a devilish grin. "Nope."

Meredith wasn't sure what she wanted more—to kiss the hell out of him or to wipe that condescending grin off his face. This was clearly a power thing. He knew something she didn't and wasn't going to share.

"You're being perverse."

Dominic shrugged. From down the hall, Meredith heard someone mock whisper, "That's so romantic."

If only they knew the truth. Dominic wasn't sweeping her away to some romantic getaway. He wasn't keeping a secret to surprise her. He was keeping a secret because he could and because he knew it would piss her off.

Reaching back inside the office, Dominic scooped up his own bag and slung it over his shoulder. Closing the door, he crowded her back into the hallway. His shoulder brushed the round curve of her breast as Meredith scrambled out of his way.

Breath backed up into her lungs, and she wobbled a little on her feet.

Her physical reaction to him irritated her. Especially when Dominic wrapped a hand around her arm, pulled her in close and brushed his lips against her ear to whisper, "You can back out. I really don't need you."

Someone close by sighed. Clearly, they hadn't heard his words but had interpreted his actions as those of a man greeting his lover.

For a brief moment, Meredith contemplated pushing him away. Telling him not to touch her.

But that would have been playing right into his hands.

Instead, she decided two could play the game. Moving into him, she placed her hand on his chest and let it drift slowly downward. Her palm settled on the curve of his hip, her fingers brushing ever so close to the fly of his pants.

Pitching her voice so that several people close could hear, she lowered her voice to a sultry tone. "There's no place I'd rather be."

A true grin played at the corners of his lips as he stared down into her doe-eyed expression.

"Be careful, angel. You're playing with fire."

Giving him a grin of her own, Meredith turned her back and tossed parting words over her shoulder, "Luckily, I'm smart enough to know how not to get burned."

He'd really hoped she wouldn't show, but he should have known better. Whenever Meredith got something in her head…she didn't let go. She was tenacious and always had been.

But right now, she was peaceful and quiet. Mostly

because she was asleep. From the moment they'd climbed the stairs into the private jet, she'd begun peppering him with questions.

The way she'd spun around, taking in the sumptuous interior of the Gulfstream he owned, a look of awe and excitement twinkling behind her eyes, had made his palms itch. He'd wanted to haul her against him and kiss the hell out of her. He wanted to be whisking her away on some romantic getaway, knowing that he'd put that expression of surprise and delight on her face.

Which was precisely why he'd put as much space between them as possible.

Dominic knew she thought he was being a pain in the ass by not telling her where they were going. But, really, he'd kept his mouth shut because they were surrounded by people who didn't need to know. The fewer people aware of their destination, the safer Tessa would be once they found her.

While they flew, Joker was in the process of doing his thing, tracking Tessa's digital footprint and trying to find clues that might help them uncover her location. And what had spooked her enough to make her run.

That's what he was focusing on, because the alternative was unimaginable.

What had started out as a necessity—keeping information tight—had become a game once they were on the plane, though. A perverse one on his part, but still… He couldn't help himself. The fire that shot through Meredith's eyes when she was irritated was intriguing.

It was the hint of real beneath the perfect exterior she tried to project to the world. And he was quickly coming to realize that's what he wanted from her.

Her real. He wanted to know the woman she was beneath the facade society and life had convinced her she needed to show. He wanted to know what pissed her off. What gave her true joy. What made her laugh. What made her sad.

She fascinated him, which probably wasn't good. Because no one—no woman—had ever fascinated him. Which was why he'd never found it difficult to let them breeze in and out of his life.

Maybe it was simply their history. Maybe it was circumstances. Maybe he needed to spend some time with her and get it out of his system. To have all the questions answered and discover Meredith wasn't any more unique than the hundreds and thousands of women he met every night at his clubs.

Beneath him, the landing gear bumped and groaned as it descended. The sound apparently disturbed Meredith, because she made a cute humming noise in the back of her throat. Stretching her arms wide over her head, she slowly pushed up to a full sit.

"What's going on?" she murmured, her voice low and smoky from sleep.

"We're getting ready to land."

Flipping her wrist over, she looked at her watch. Even sleepy and sluggish, he watched as her brain calculated the time they'd been in the air against possible places they could be landing.

"Probably not somewhere in the US."

"No."

Turning in her seat, Meredith raked him with those bright blue eyes that always made him think of a summer sky filled with sunshine. "Are you going to make me guess? There are a lot of places in the world to cover, and we've been in the air for a pretty long time."

She'd figure it out soon enough. "Paris."

Meredith's eyes widened. "Good thing I grabbed my passport."

It was, although it wouldn't have been an issue. Money and status solved many things.

Reaching beside her, Meredith flipped up the shade that had been drawn over the window and pressed her nose to the glass. "I've never been to Paris."

Dominic couldn't stop the tug of satisfaction at his gut or his lips. It wasn't often he'd seen Meredith excited, and even though she was trying to tamp it down, he heard it in her voice. It was difficult not to feel a sense of satisfaction that something he'd done had put that tone there.

"I wish we weren't here for such a concerning reason."

"I'll bring you back sometime when we can enjoy all the city has to offer." The words were out of his mouth before he'd even registered them in his brain.

Why the hell would he make that kind of offer when he had no intention of keeping it?

Meredith turned to look at him. Her eyebrow lifted as she searched his face before silently turning back to the spread of the city finally coming into focus.

That was her only response to what he'd said. She didn't scoff. She didn't accept. She simply ignored him and instead concentrated on what was before them.

And in that moment, Dominic realized he did want to come back here with her. And not simply because she obviously would enjoy it. But because she didn't think he would.

What the hell was going on with him?

"What's our first move?"

Shaking the unexpected response away, Dominic focused on what Meredith was asking.

"We'll stop by the apartment she was staying in. See if we can find anything there. Talk to the neighbors, although she wasn't here very long. See if we can uncover any leads."

He'd also check in with Joker to see if he'd found anything useful while they were in the air.

The plane touched down on the tarmac. Meredith didn't wait before she jumped from her seat and reached for the bag that had been stowed in a compartment at the front of the cabin.

She was standing at the door, patiently waiting,

when they rolled to a stop and the flight attendant arrived to open the door so they could disembark.

Grabbing his own bag, Dominic followed slowly behind her. This was going to be a long few days.

Ten

As much as she would have loved to explore Paris—the city was gorgeous and everything she'd ever imagined—they had things to do, and this wasn't a vacation.

It was midmorning when they arrived, and Dominic immediately took control. He sent their bags off in one car, no doubt to wherever they were staying. He ushered her to another, placing a single hand at the small of her back as he held the door open before following her inside.

Nope, a ripple effect of heat and awareness didn't spread from the point where he'd touched. Not at all.

Meredith used the cityscape out the window to distract herself as the car weaved in and out of the city. She shouldn't have been surprised when Dominic spoke fluent French, obviously communicating with their driver about where they were going. But she was.

"You speak French." It wasn't a question, because clearly he did.

"I speak French, Spanish and enough Mandarin to be dangerous."

Growing up, Meredith had often heard Annalise complain about Dominic and his lack of care where school was concerned. In some ways, his sister had taken on the role of mother, fussing over him and attempting to ensure he did what he was supposed to. Which, as anyone could imagine, hadn't gone over very well. Dominic didn't appreciate rules or feel the need to live up to expectations.

Because of that, Meredith had always assumed he hadn't done very well in school. She knew for a fact he hadn't finished college but dropped out halfway through to work at the club in Magnifique and two years later opened Excess.

"Why?" It was an honest question fueled by real curiosity. It wasn't like he lived a lifestyle that required him to know those languages.

A knowing smile played at Dominic's lips. "Because I enjoy learning them. And I have business in regions that speak the languages. I don't like being at a disadvantage or relying on someone else to translate for me. Especially when business is involved."

She should have known. It was a control thing. But in this case, it was difficult not to be impressed with his drive, ambition and intelligence.

"I'm impressed."

He laughed, but the sound had an unexpected edge to it. "Because I can learn a language or that I bothered to take the time to do it?"

Meredith shrugged. "Both. Don't play the af-fronted card, Dominic. I'm starting to realize you've cultivated an image that might not actually be real. I've always known you were good at what you do, but I'm also coming to understand there's much more to you than the devil-may-care, charismatic party boy you pretend to be."

This time, the grin that split his face was full of humor. Leaning into the space between them, Dom-inic brought his face close and leveled her a drill-ing stare. "Don't tell anyone. You'll screw with a good thing."

"You'd rather people believe that you care about nothing more than fun, entertainment and sex."

"I do care about fun, entertainment—" he reached out and ran the pad of his index finger over the line of her jaw, her throat and into the open V of her shirt "—and I'm damn serious about sex."

Meredith swallowed. She wanted him to keep going. Wanted him to rip the buttons off her shirt and put his mouth where his finger had been. She wanted more of what they'd shared several days ago.

Her body burned for it.

And if the blazing heat in his eyes was any indi-cation, so did he.

Meredith opened her mouth to tell him to keep

going. To beg him for more. But the sudden stop of the car jolted her back to reality.

From the front seat, the gentleman driving rattled off a fast-paced sentence. Dominic responded with what were obviously instructions and a hand gesture that clearly indicated he wanted their driver to wait.

Opening the door, Dominic alighted onto the sidewalk in front of a nondescript building. Reaching a hand back inside, he helped her out behind him.

Meredith looked around. Clearly, they were in the middle of a neighborhood of sorts. The buildings were each five or six stories high. Row houses or apartments, it was difficult to tell. They'd left behind the hustle and bustle of the more commercial and touristy areas of the city and all the people that came with them.

Here, there was a sense of quiet. Of calm. Down the street a woman walked with two small children and a little dog. From somewhere farther away, Meredith heard the faint sound of children laughing. The air was crisp and clear.

Still holding her hand, Dominic urged her to follow him inside the building. Through the front door, there was a desk with a gentleman standing guard behind it.

Dominic spearheaded the conversation, and after several minutes, they were shown to an elevator and allowed to go up. The doors shut, closing them into the small space.

Meredith didn't turn to look at him but continued

to stare at the shiny silver wall as she asked, "What did you tell him?"

"I told him the truth. I own the apartment upstairs and we've come to visit the friend who rents it from us."

"You own the apartment?" He said he'd told the truth, but had he really?

"Well, one of the businesses I own—co-own—does."

The way he said it made Meredith suspect that finding his actual name anywhere on a deed or mortgage would be next to impossible. But that he still technically owned the place.

"You've used this apartment before?"

"No, we've had it for some time, though. It was rented out until several months ago."

"You're part of a real estate management company?"

Dominic smiled at the door but didn't share his humor with her. "Something like that."

She could see how that might be a valuable asset when you were relocating people who needed a safe place to live as they started over.

The elevator opened onto a long hallway. There were only four doors along it, though, indicating the apartments that hid behind were rather large. Dominic stopped at the last one, punched a number into the digital keypad that locked the door and then pushed it open when the mechanism gave with a whir and a click.

Stepping inside, Meredith wasn't entirely certain

what to expect. The space was a combination of modern and classic. Open concept mixed with bare brick walls. The kitchen area was sleek with dark gray cabinets, black metal finishes, white marble and tile. The living area contained a turquoise leather sectional with square arms and a squat profile.

It was clean, welcoming and somehow still absolutely bare. Like the person who lived there hadn't imparted any of their own personality into the space. Yet.

Looking around, Meredith tried to find any clue that Tessa had even been there. No fruit in the bowl sitting atop the black dining table. No magazines or books carelessly tossed onto the coffee table. No dishes left in the sink to tackle later.

Dominic crossed to the single hallway to the left of the living space and popped open the three doors along the way. Meredith followed, sticking her head into the spare bedroom, guest bath and finally the master suite.

Along the way, it was much the same. Nothing.

Dominic didn't bother to tiptoe around. He went right for the attached closet and flung open the door. When he disappeared inside the walk-in, Meredith decided the space might be big, but she really didn't want to crowd into it with him.

Instead, she chose the second door, the attached bath. Clearly, the apartment had been renovated at some point, combining history and old-world charm with modern conveniences. A large soaker tub sat at the far end of the space, next to a glass-walled shower big enough for five people to occupy at once.

A long double vanity took up the opposite wall. Crossing to it, Meredith started opening drawers.

"Nothing. Not a single thing of hers in the closet. We stocked the apartment before she came. Every piece of clothing is gone."

Meredith turned. "Same in here. The drawers are all empty. Not a tube of gloss or mascara or tooth-paste."

Something caught the corner of Meredith's eye, though, as her gaze swept across the space. A small trash can tucked beneath the edge of the counter. Leaning down, she grabbed it and set it on the counter. Peering inside, she found several boxes and wrappers.

Clearly, someone had opened a lot of new prod-ucts and hadn't bothered emptying the evidence be-fore leaving.

"She was here."

"How do you know?"

Fishing gingerly through everything, Meredith pulled out a box with a pastel floral background. "Because this is the brand of perfume Tessa has used since we were in high school. It just happens to be French."

Spinning on his heel, Dominic raked fingers through his mahogany hair. He looked at the room one more time and then strode out to do the same with the rest of the apartment.

If it wasn't for Meredith's find in the master bath, it would seem no one had occupied the space at all.

"You have good observation skills," he finally said, knowing that she'd followed him even without turning to see her.

"Looking through the trash is hardly an earth-shattering breakthrough of intelligence."

She might be right, but he certainly hadn't thought to do it. Although maybe he would have eventually.

"On the plus side, there's no evidence of a struggle. No overturned furniture, knocked-over vases or scattered magazines on the floor."

Once again, Meredith was right. In fact, "Everything is perfectly in its place." A trademark trait for a lot of abuse victims. It was often a way for them to control a part of the environment when they had no control over other aspects of their lives.

"Someone who'd come to take her back wouldn't bother to pack all her clothes and toiletries."

"True," Dominic said. Grim comfort considering Tessa was still missing. "Something spooked her, though."

Meredith agreed, nodding. "She ran."

It was an accurate guess, all things considered. "The question is why?" Dominic spun, slower this time, searching for any clue that might help.

There just weren't any.

Meredith slowly did the same, coming back to face him with a grim expression pulling at her mouth. "The more important question is where the heck did she go?"

Since the apartment provided them with no clues, they agreed to speak to the neighbors. But Tessa had only been there a very short time, so it was likely they hadn't even met her yet, let alone seen anything useful.

Several hours later, Dominic's fears were realized. No one in the building had been able to provide them any help. Empty-handed and getting more concerned by the moment, he called their driver to take them to the hotel.

On the drive, Nic checked in with Joker, giving him the rundown on what they'd found. Or rather, the lack of what they'd found.

Tessa had been given cash, a new identity and all the documents attached to it, including credit cards. However, according to Joker, none of the cards had been used. But that wasn't surprising given she'd had a crash course on staying off the grid and had plenty of liquid funds at her disposal.

It might take them days or weeks to find her. Which didn't sit well with Dominic. The unsettling pit in his stomach said she was in trouble.

But more personally, the idea of spending the next several weeks traipsing across Europe with Meredith… it was dangerous on so many levels. Especially now that his memory kept replaying the sight, sound and taste of her.

He knew what they could have together.

He also knew that if he gave in, they'd both regret it. Meredith would want more from him, more than he could give.

Not for the first time, he wondered what it would take to convince her to head home. He also thought briefly about simply putting her in a car with instructions to take her to the airport and ensure she got on a plane.

But he figured that wouldn't go over well.

Besides, she really had been a help in searching the apartment and had the investigative background he might need. Better to stick things out for now. He could keep his hands to himself. Outside of that one slip, he'd been doing it for years where she was concerned.

Meredith tried not to be impressed. The hotel suite Dominic had booked was unbelievable. Hell, there was a baby grand piano sitting in the middle of one of the rooms. Who needed a piano when they were on vacation?

But, really, it was the view that took her breath away.

Night had fallen and, after stowing the few things she'd packed into her carry-on, Meredith had been left with nothing to occupy her hands or mind.

Which had only made her worry.

Wandering back into the main living area, she walked up to the wall of windows overlooking the city. Across the street there was a small restaurant, the kind that only held a handful of patrons but had twelve or so tables scattered along the sidewalk.

Candles burned, people laughed and wine flowed freely. Couples strolled along the cobblestone street, and in the distance, the Eiffel Tower twinkled against the darkened sky.

It was magical, and part of her was dying to slip downstairs and explore. But the rest of her felt guilty for wanting to indulge while her friend was most likely scared and alone.

Not that sitting up here all night was likely to change that.

Meredith had just about convinced herself it wouldn't be selfish to take an hour or two when Dominic strode into the room. His steps faltered when he realized she was there, but only for a moment.

His gaze swept over her, taking in the ripped jeans and oversize shirt she'd changed into. When he reached her naked feet, a single eyebrow winged up, and the corner of his lips tipped into a barely there grin.

"What?" Meredith asked, her tone defensive.

"Nothing."

She made a sound in the back of her throat. "Your expression says otherwise."

Shrugging, Dominic headed for the full kitchen at the far end of the open area. "I just wouldn't have pegged you for the sparkly blue polish type, is all."

Meredith glanced down at her toes, wiggling them against the soft carpet. "What's wrong with sparkly and blue?"

"Nothing."

Why did she care what he thought about her pedicure? She didn't. Not really. So why did she ask, "What color would you expect?"

"Oh, nude. Pale pink. If you're feeling really froggy, maybe a nice apple red. Something safe."

Meredith tried not to rise to the bait he was clearly setting. They were talking about her polish color, not the plight of third world countries. But somehow she couldn't let it go.

"Safe, huh? Maybe you don't really know me as well as you think you do."

This time, the smile he sent her glittered temptingly out of those dark green eyes. "Clearly. But I find it sad that the only place you let yourself be a little daring is with your toenail polish, something most people will never actually see."

She wanted to growl at him. To argue that he was the one being silly by distilling her entire personality down to this one thing.

Unable to stop herself, Meredith followed him into the kitchen. "I take risks every day, Dominic. My work requires it. And I sure as hell took one with you the other night."

This time, when he turned to her, he used his height and those damn broad shoulders to crowd her. Arching away, Meredith pressed the small of her back into the edge of the counter and blinked up at him.

Her heart hammered against her ribs. Dominic planted those wide, capable palms on either side of her hips, blocking her in. Leaning close, the heat of his words brushed against the side of her throat.

"That wasn't a risk, Meredith. That was combustion that neither of us could stop."

Before she could respond, he jerked away. Grateful for the counter that was holding her up, Meredith sagged against it. Blood rushed through her body, audible in her own ears. And the pulse of her centered right between her thighs, an incessant cadence that taunted her.

Because God help her, she wanted more. He made her burn with nothing more than words and memories. He hadn't even touched her, and her entire body felt like it was on fire.

While he puttered around in the refrigerator, seemingly unaffected by what he'd just said and done.

Bastard.

Eleven

Dominic was hungry, and not necessarily for the food he was about to prepare. But it was either busy his hands with something productive or bury them in Meredith's cloud of red-gold hair and kiss the hell out of her.

He was opting for the safe choice.

Now who was being risk averse?

Shaking his head, Dominic pulled out the ingredients he needed to make a meal. It would have been easy to throw something simple together, but he rather hoped something more complicated would absorb his concentration.

He liked cooking. It soothed something inside him and always had. He enjoyed watching ingredi-

ents come together into a dish that could excite and
nourish at the same time.

But not even chopping, searing or the heat from
the stove could distract him from the fact that Meredith sat on the other side of the island, silently watching him.

Judging him. As she always had.

Part of him wished she'd just go away, find something else to entertain her. Hell, they had an amazing city spread out at their feet…which was precisely
why he'd opted to stay in.

Because he knew he wouldn't be able to let her
explore Paris alone. She'd never been to the city, and
while he had no doubt she was capable of taking care
of herself, he wasn't the kind of man who left women
unprotected…even if they didn't feel they needed
someone to keep watch.

Add Paris and Meredith together…there was simply something about the atmosphere in the city that
would stretch his already strained control.

The silence grew between them, broken only by
the hiss of meat against heated steel and the sharp
snick of his blade connecting with the cutting board.

"Where'd you learn to handle that knife?"

Dominic looked up from the vegetables he was ju-
lienning, taking in Meredith's studied gaze. The way
her chin rested in the cup of her palm. Oh, she was
absolutely watching him. But he'd already known
that. Could feel the weight of her gaze as he'd moved.

"I spent a lot of time in my dad's casino."

"Which doesn't explain that," Meredith said,

waving at the cutting board and the perfectly sliced veggies.

"The casino includes quite a few restaurants, bars and clubs. All of which serve food. I had a lot of time on my hands and energy to spare. My dad believed that while Annalise and I had access to everything money could provide, we still needed to understand the value of working to earn what we had. And he wanted us to understand every aspect of the casino for when we took over. He put us to work in the various businesses when we were in our teens. I spent a lot of time in the kitchens."

Meredith nodded. "I knew Annalise had spent time learning the casino side of things, but I always thought that was because she *wanted* to learn."

"She did. She was always drawn to that aspect of the business."

"But not you?"

Dominic shrugged. "It was hers. I found other things that interested me."

"Like the club."

He could hear the derision in Meredith's voice and couldn't help the twisted, derisive smile that pulled at his lips. "What do you have against my clubs?"

"Nothing."

"Bullshit."

Meredith sighed. Standing up, she crossed to one of the cabinets, pulled down a wineglass and then poured herself a healthy dose of red from the bottle he'd opened on the counter. He'd planned to let it breathe and serve it with dinner, but…

He half expected her to walk back to her seat. To put the island firmly between them. Instead, she leaned her hips against the edge and sipped.

"No, really. I don't have a problem with your clubs."

"Then your problem is with me." He didn't bother making the statement a question. It was something he'd always known.

Her luscious lips tugged into a soft frown. "No, my problem is with me."

This time, when Dominic looked up from his task, he took the time to study her face. The confusion and disappointment that pulled at her features.

For the first time, Dominic wondered if those negative emotions she was always throwing his way had more to do with her than with her opinion of him. For some reason, that made him both hopeful and sad.

"Explain."

"You're good at what you do. Obviously, considering you have clubs all over the world and your bank account is rather healthy, even without the benefit of your family's money."

Why did her words sound more like an accusation than the praise they were supposed to be?

"I know your security is top-notch and you protect the people in your clubs to the best of your ability." She let out a quiet laugh. "I've seen it with my own eyes."

"True."

"I had a friend who was slipped a date-rape drug at a club when we were in college. I've never forgotten how frightened I was when I couldn't find her. Or the devastation she experienced after she woke up and realized what had happened."

Dominic's belly clenched. "I hate that that happened to your friend, but her experience has nothing to do with Excess. Or me."

Dominic scraped the vegetables from the cutting board into the sizzling pan on the stove and started gathering the ingredients for a garlic cream sauce.

"I know. Which is why I said it was a me problem."

The corners of Dominic's lips tugged downward. "You say that, but I can hear it in your voice anytime you talk about what I do for a living. You judge and look down on me with disdain. Have for a long time."

Meredith opened her mouth, the protest clear in those pale blue eyes, but she shut it again before responding. The sharp pink tip of her tongue swiped across her bottom lip, leaving a glistening trail he had to struggle not to lean over and follow with his own lips.

Finally, she tried again. "It's easier that way."

"How?"

This time, Meredith stalled by taking a sip of her wine. He watched her chin tip backward, exposing the long column of her throat. She was testing him. Seriously. The memory of the taste of her skin bloomed across the back of his tongue.

He wanted that a hell of a lot more than the fragrant meal he was currently preparing.

"Easier to hold you at arm's length if I convince

myself I don't like you. Don't agree with the way you live your life."

Slowly, deliberately, Dominic set the spoon he'd been using onto the counter beside him. His hands curled into tight fists. "Why do you need to hold me at arm's length?"

Holding the glass in front of her chest like a piece of armor, Meredith looked at him. He could see the conflict in her eyes. The swirl of need, the fear and anticipation.

"You know why," she finally whispered.

Reaching behind him, Dominic blindly flicked the knobs on the stove, turning all the burners to off. At the same time, he reached for the glass, plucking it out of her fingers to set it gently on the counter beside her.

"Tell me anyway."

Hands empty, she filled them with him instead. Reaching, she wrapped one hand around his hip and the other around the base of his neck. Tugged. She didn't have to urge too hard before he followed.

His hips pressed against hers. She was soft everywhere he was hard. Her body yielded to his, accepting him.

"I want you. I've always wanted you. You're the man who haunts my dreams, Nic. You're the man who can make my blood sing with nothing more than a simple brush of his fingers across my skin. You make me mad. You make me want. You make me burn with a need that terrifies me, because I can't control it."

Dominic completely understood. For her, letting go with him would be the ultimate leap of faith. Just like for him, allowing her to see behind the mask he'd painstakingly built over the years, scared the shit out of him.

Tonight, the need for her outweighed that fear.

Reaching for her, Dominic lifted her up. Meredith wrapped her legs around his waist, clinging to him in a way that made him feel powerful.

"Thank God. You're not alone," he growled before striding through the suite.

She should have known this was exactly where they were going to end up.

And, honestly, hadn't she? Wasn't that the reason she'd been trying to put distance between them since getting on that plane?

But it was useless. She wanted him, more each time they were together. And not simply because of some nebulous physical attraction—although that was definitely there—but because she was seriously starting to like the man.

He surprised her. He pissed her off and challenged her. He made her proud to know him. He was a good man beneath the charm and devil-may-care attitude.

And, God, he could make her body sing.

His strong hands cupped her bottom, pressing her tight against his body. With each powerful stride, her body jolted and her throbbing core rubbed tantalizingly against the long ridge of his erection.

Pressing her lips to his throat, Meredith licked

and kissed and sucked at his skin. He tasted of salt and sin.

His hands might be occupied, but hers were free, and she took full advantage of the situation. Reaching to the center of his back, she tugged at his shirt, pulling it up as they went.

Miles of gorgeous, tanned skin became her playground.

Last time, she'd been a bit overwhelmed and hadn't taken the time to appreciate and enjoy him. This time, she was dead set on getting the most out of this experience. She wanted all of him.

Her hands raced over his shoulders, chest and ribs. Her mouth followed, taking in as much as she could from her limited position. Latching her mouth onto the pounding pulse at his throat, Meredith sucked at the same time her fingers found the tight nub of his nipple and tugged.

Dominic made an aching, growling sound in the back of his throat. "Be careful, angel," he muttered, his own mouth busy licking across her skin.

Feeling bold, she taunted, "Or what?"

They entered the main bedroom, the one he'd told her to take when they'd first walked in. A single lamp on the nightstand glowed with a soft, golden light, illuminating the center of the bed even as the rest of the room remained dark.

Using his hold on her legs, Dominic flipped her backward onto the bed. Her body bounced before settling straight in the center.

"Or I'm going to enjoy torturing you. Making you beg. How many orgasms do you think you can take?"

Meredith's sex throbbed. It wasn't just his words that had her body flooding with anticipation and need. No, it was the expression on his face. The burning heat of his gaze. All that banked intensity focused solely on her.

Yes, she wanted all that. She wanted all of him.

But she wasn't ready to give in. Just yet.

"Please, we both know you were going to delight in making me beg anyway."

Lifting up on one elbow, Meredith reached for the buttons that ran the length of her shirt. Slowly, she flicked them open, one at a time. She reveled in the way his sharp gaze watched, following the ever-widening line of skin that she exposed.

Spreading both sides of her shirt open, she slowly trailed a single finger across her body. Following the strap of her bra over her shoulder. The line of ribs to circle her belly button. Brushing just beneath the edge of her pants. Over the curve of lace across the mound of her breast.

Dipping beneath the fabric, Meredith found the tightened bud of her own nipple and squeezed. Heat flared deep in Dominic's blazing eyes.

"Touch me, Nic."

He didn't wait for another demand. Reaching for the opening of her jeans, he released the button and zipper before tugging them down her thighs.

The hot brand of his mouth followed, leaving kisses, licks and the delicate mark of teeth along her waist, hips and inner thighs. But he wasn't done as he tossed the clothing to the floor.

Oh, no.

Grasping her legs, Dominic pulled her to the edge of the bed even as he dropped to his knees. Palms to her thighs, he urged her to open as his mouth trailed high. Right to the center of her aching body.

Without breaking eye contact, Dominic flicked out his tongue and tasted her. The heat that he caused, the need of him, was too much.

Dropping her head back, Meredith let out a strangled groan of pleasure as sensations bombarded her.

His lips and tongue teased. Licked. Laved. Sucked. He drove her wild, bringing her to the brink of release only to back off and barely touch. Need pounded through her blood, an incessant cadence centered right at her aching sex.

"Please," she finally breathed out, unable to take it. "Please, Nic."

Her body writhed, searching, needing. But his hands held her steady, keeping her exactly where he wanted as he prolonged the torture.

Until she'd had enough. Rearing up, Meredith buried her hands in his hair and held his mouth to her. Grinding her hips against him, she took what she needed.

And he watched, his fiery gaze steady on hers. Her eyelids were heavy, her neck barely capable of holding her head up. But she couldn't look away. The command, the dare in his gaze wouldn't let her break the connection.

Not even as the orgasm ripped through her. Her entire body pulsed and shuddered. But he pushed her for more. Using the flat of his tongue, he worked her until the first orgasm exploded into another.

Finally, Meredith collapsed back on the bed. Unable to take any more, she used her heels to push away from his torturous, perfect, pleasure-giving mouth.

Twelve

God, she was gorgeous. Dominic couldn't get enough of her. Enough of her pleasure. Enough of the sounds she made in the back of her throat. The whimpers, moans and little mewling.

He could watch her orgasm all night. Hell, he had half a mind to do just that.

But his own body had other ideas.

The need to feel her heat wrapped tight around him throbbed through him.

He enjoyed sex. A hell of a lot. But nothing compared to what he experienced with Meredith. With other women, it had been a mutual search for gratification. She got hers, he got his. With Meredith, while his balls might want to kill him, knowing he'd given her pleasure was almost enough.

Almost.

Taking the time to shed his jeans and shorts while Meredith took a little breather, Dominic climbed onto the bed. Straddling her hips, he leaned down and began running soft, slow kisses across her body.

God, her skin was so pale and perfect. Silky and smooth.

He relished the way her breath caught behind her ribs when he tugged gently at her distended nipples. Slowly, her eyes blinked open. A half smile curled at the edges of her lips as she looked up at him out of glassy, unfocused eyes.

"I'm pretty sure you broke me."

Dominic chuckled. "I'm pretty sure I didn't."

Reaching for him, her hands were a little less than steady as they ran down the length of his body. Energy skated just beneath his skin wherever she touched.

Cupping his face, Meredith gently tugged him down until his mouth touched hers.

The kiss was easy, light. For a few heartbeats. Her lips opened, and the tip of her tongue stroked deep inside, mirroring exactly what he wanted to do with her body. Meredith undulated beneath him, rubbing her hips and breasts against him.

Spreading her thighs, she cupped his hips and urged him down.

"I want you, Nic. I want to feel you, stroking deep inside me. I want to feel you come apart in my arms."

God, he wanted that, too.

And she didn't have to tell him twice.

Positioning the head of his sheathed cock at the entrance to her body, Dominic lifted her hips and thrust deep.

Meredith's eyes fluttered, and a sigh of pleasure ghosted through her parted lips.

Nope, that wasn't going to work for him.

"Look at me." He wanted to watch her eyes go hazy with pleasure. And he wanted her to watch him. Know he was the one making her body sing.

Meredith obeyed, her gaze locking with his. He started with long, slow strokes. In and out. Over and over as ecstasy built between them.

"You feel so damn good," he groaned. "Perfect."

Meredith shook her head but didn't say anything.

Not then, and not as the tempo built. She moved with him, thrusting and reaching. Searching for that ultimate moment together.

It wasn't long before a frenzy took over. Before he could feel the orgasm building at the base of his spine, relentless even as he tried to hold it back. This was too good. He wasn't ready for it to end.

But when Meredith's release slammed into her, the tight clasp of her body milking him was too much. The orgasm exploded through him, a rush of pleasure and perfection. Everything around him dimmed to nothing except for Meredith's blue eyes. The solid, steady, flawless depths grasped him. Held him. Wouldn't let go.

Something deep inside Dominic's chest exploded right along with the rest of his body. There was an ache…and then peace.

Collapsing beside her, Dominic was careful not to crush her with the weight of his body. But he also wanted to feel her. Wanted the shared rise and fall of their labored breaths.

They stayed that way, wrapped together for several quiet moments.

Normally, this was about the time Dominic started getting antsy. He'd never found enjoyment in cuddling. But right now, he had no intention of letting Meredith go.

After a little while, she stirred. At first, he was afraid she was the one eager to break their connection, but instead, she rolled onto her side and snuggled down into the shelter of his body.

Running a hand over her hair, he said, "Get some sleep."

She nodded, her head rubbing against his naked shoulder, before murmuring, "Are you going to be here when I wake up?"

Her question gutted him. Not just the words, but the innocent hope that ran beneath them. And the realization that he'd hurt her when he hadn't meant to.

The last thing he'd ever want to do was hurt her. Hell, he'd spent years avoiding her so he could prevent that very thing.

Pressing his lips to her hair, he whispered, "I'm not going anywhere, angel."

Meredith woke slowly, awareness seeping in. Without thought, she reached a hand to the bed beside her. The feel of cold sheets jolted that contented, languid sensation right out of her.

Sitting up, she grasped the sheet to her naked chest. Her eyes wheeled around the room, taking in the semidarkness that the blackout curtains across the windows provided.

What time was it?

Bright sunlight crept through the cracks at the edges, so it had to be pretty late.

And Dominic was gone again.

Dammit, would she never learn?

Vaulting out of bed, Meredith scooped up a shirt off the floor and tugged it over her head even as she padded for the door. Yanking it open, she stalked down the hallway and came to an abrupt stop when she slammed into the sight waiting for her in the middle of the open living area.

Dominic, jeans slung low on his hips and his gloriously naked back to her, stood at the wall of windows looking out over the city. One hand held a phone to his ear while the other was balled into a fist in his pocket.

That fist managed to pull the worn denim tight across the curve of his delectable ass.

Relief washed through her, riding right behind the sudden urge to take a bite out of the target he was unwittingly giving her.

She was so distracted by the vision of him that the tension in his body didn't immediately register. Until she realized he was bouncing on the balls of his feet, a virtual bundle of vibrating energy.

"Yeah, man. I understand," he said. "We'll head that way in half an hour."

His silence clearly indicated conversation from whoever was on the other end of the phone call. Stepping closer, Meredith fought the urge to set a stilling hand on his waist.

And then she realized there was no reason not to go with what her gut was telling her to do.

When she touched him, she half expected him to jump. Instead, he leaned into her hand. Meredith's heart gave a little jolt at the easy way he responded to her gesture. Rolling up onto her toes, she pressed the length of her body to his and settled a soft kiss to the stark edge of his shoulder blade.

His free hand slipped out of that pocket. Fingers unfurling, he grasped her own, linking his hand with hers and pulling her tighter against him.

"I know she's likely still moving, but at least it's a place to start. We have the direction she's traveling in now. Let Stone know and bring in some of the other staff. See if you can make an educated guess as to where her next destination might be."

Dominic hummed in the back of his throat before hanging up the call without saying goodbye.

"Is that a guy thing?"

"What?"

"Just hanging up."

Dominic shrugged. "Maybe. Joker got a hit on Tessa."

His words should have made Meredith happy, but the fact that his tone was still troubled meant that she couldn't take the news as a victory. Because, clearly, it wasn't.

"Where is she?"

"Well, she was in Marseille. A day and a half ago."

"You don't think she's still there." She didn't bother making it a question, because it was clear he didn't.

"Don't know, but I'm operating on the assumption she isn't. We'll head that way, though. We can get there in a few hours."

Nodding, Meredith started to drop her arms from their perch on Dominic's waist, but his grip on her fingers tightened, keeping her in place.

Twisting, Dominic used his hold to bring her hands behind her back. Pressing their entwined fingers into the arch of her spine, he urged her closer. Dipping down, his mouth found hers in a kiss that had her drowning in mere seconds.

Oh was about the only thing Meredith's mind could process.

The kiss wasn't just heat, although that was part of it. It was welcome. It was apology. And so much more.

Breath backed up into Meredith's lungs, but she didn't care. Who needed to breathe? Her body turned liquid, melting against him.

Pulling back, he murmured, "Good morning," before greeting her with another touch of his lips.

"Morning," she mumbled against the teasing, tempting brush of his mouth.

Her body buzzed with excitement and energy, which wasn't unusual when Dominic was around. In her head, Meredith calculated. Surely they had time for a quickie before heading out.

But before she could make a move in that direction, Dominic spun her around and connected the flat of his palm to the curve of her half-naked ass.

Meredith yelped with surprise and stumbled forward from the unexpected tap. Her skin tingled, warmth spreading out across her rear, somehow finding purchase at the center of her sex.

She should be irritated he'd just smacked her ass. But for some reason, she wasn't. In fact, she wanted him to do it again.

But she didn't necessarily want him to know that.

Craning her neck around, Meredith sent him a scowl. "What the hell?"

A half smirk pulled at Dominic's mouth. "Angel, don't even try to pretend you don't want me to do that again. The little sound you made in the back of your throat, the glitter of heat in those soul-destroying blue eyes and the flush of awareness spreading across your delectable skin are all giving you away."

Meredith's eyes narrowed. "Someone woke up with an inflated ego."

The playful smirk dropped from his expression. In one huge stride, Dominic closed the space between them. Wrapping his large palm around the base of her neck, he tipped her backward. She expected another kiss. Instead, she got something even more devastating.

And hopeful.

"Angel, I woke up next to you and promise there isn't anywhere else I'd rather be." For several seconds, his intense, powerful gaze searched her own. Looking for evidence that she believed him?

Meredith's body was frozen—she couldn't have moved even if she'd wanted to. God, this man was going to be her undoing. He wasn't what she'd expected.

He was so much more. Which scared the hell out of her.

But not enough to walk away.

His playful smirk returned. Taking her hand, Dominic pressed it against the fly of his jeans. "The only thing inflated around you, angel, is this."

An approving hum buzzed through her throat. Meredith squeezed and then slowly ran her palm down the solid length of him. Denim scraped against her hand. It would be nothing to pull down the zipper since the button on his fly was already undone.

To hold the warm, smooth heat of him. Her palms itched to do just that.

But he must have read her intentions, because Dominic jerked his hips back. "Nope, as much as I'd love to see what that devious brain of yours is thinking, we don't have time."

A pout tugged at Meredith's lips. She never pouted. About anything. What was this man doing to her?

Whispering in her ear, he finished with, "For now."

The blatant promise in those words had a shiver

of need and anticipation ripping through her body. "I'm going to hold you to that promise."

"God, I hope so. Now, go pack."

This time their luck was a little better. Joker told them Tessa had used one of her new credit cards to rent a room for a single night. Apparently, the boutique hotel refused to take cash—security purposes or something. And when he and Meredith arrived at the hotel to question the owner, she was rather forthcoming with information.

Good for them, but bad if someone else was following Tessa. Luckily, they had knowledge that made tracking her purchase easier than it would be for anyone else.

And the owner, a woman in her early fifties with salt-and-pepper hair pulled up into a tight twist and eyes that were wide and watchful, told them no one else had asked about Tessa.

"She kept to herself. Didn't go anywhere and asked to have dinner delivered to her room." The woman shrugged. "Who comes to Marseille and doesn't experience the city? I thought it strange."

He bet she had.

"She was here alone?" Meredith asked. "No one visited her? Asked about her?"

"*Non*, no one was with her." The woman paused. "She did seem rather…antsy, though, as she was checking in. Looking behind her at the door. I just thought she was a weird, flighty American."

The way she said it made Dominic think she dealt

with weird Americans often and took the eccentricity for granted.

"When did she leave?" Meredith asked.

"Hmm, she checked out yesterday morning. Early, actually. Around seven."

They'd gained a couple days. "Did she happen to mention where she was going?"

"*Non*. In fact, she was very evasive when I asked her. I was just making small talk, you know, trying to offer suggestions if she didn't have any plans in mind. But she wouldn't tell me. Said she didn't have a specific destination, was going to decide once she reached the train station."

Meredith took care of thanking the owner while Dominic strode outside. Connecting a call to Joker, he relayed what little information they'd gotten before dropping his cell back into his pocket.

Standing on the sidewalk, staring out at the people bustling by in the city, he couldn't help the rock of worry and frustration that sat in his belly, growing with each passing hour. A sense of doom that just wouldn't let go.

"I don't even know where to start," he finally said, putting voice to the frustration.

Meredith's hand landed on his arm, a silent offer of support that he hadn't realized he needed until right now. "We might not have much, but we have more than we started with. She said Tessa was heading to the train station."

"If Tessa was telling the truth. She might have

been putting up a smoke screen for anyone following her tracks."

"Maybe, but what if she wasn't? What if she was trying to be careful but accidentally let slip a tiny detail? It's worth checking. Besides, what else are we going to do?"

She had a point. Joker was working his magic, and while they waited to see if anything else popped… they could at least run down the single lead they had, even if it was unlikely to yield anything.

Grabbing a taxi, they headed for the train station. Dominic found himself peering at every woman who walked past, trying to find Tessa in the crowd even though she was likely long gone.

Inside the doorway, Meredith paused, her eyes scanning the building. Dominic watched as her calculating gaze took everything in. He could practically see her mind spinning, weighing, dismissing and trying to pick up any thread that could help.

"She said she was going to decide where to go once she arrived. What if her plan was to buy a ticket for the first train leaving?"

If Tessa had come to the station, it made good sense. She wouldn't want to stay in any place very long, not if she was afraid someone was on her heels.

"Yeah, that's not a bad assumption."

Picking up his phone, Dominic tapped out a text to Joker. He'd be able to access the schedule from yesterday and make an educated guess about which train Tessa might have taken.

Five minutes later an answering text pinged into

his phone. "According to Joker there are two possibilities. A train that left at 7:50 a.m. heading back to Paris. And another leaving at 8:05 a.m. for Monte Carlo."

Together, they both said, "Monte Carlo."

"She wouldn't head back to where she'd just come from, right?"

Dominic shook his head. Probably not, although there was no way of knowing for certain. Part of him hated to leave the one place they knew she'd been for a hunch, but she wasn't in Marseille any longer. Of that he was certain.

Rushing over to the ticket window, he bought two tickets for the next train to Monte Carlo, and together, they went to wait.

Thirteen

Meredith had never been to Monte Carlo. Hell, it had never crossed her mind that she'd find herself in Monaco. Life was strange sometimes.

But the city was gorgeous, nestled between the beautiful blue Mediterranean on one side and the Alps on the other. Awe inspiring and breathtaking. The atmosphere was completely different than in Paris, luxurious and exciting.

But they weren't there to indulge at the casino or drive fast race cars.

Meredith couldn't shake the tight, itchy feeling that centered at the back of her neck. From the moment they'd stepped off the train, she'd had to fight off the sensation of being watched.

But each time she turned, the only people who

greeted her were others rushing to their destinations, preoccupied with their own purposes.

Outside the station, Dominic pulled her off to the side. Glancing around, Meredith asked, "Now what?"

He frowned and let his own gaze scan the area around them. "I'm honestly not sure. I was hoping Joker would've called back by now."

Meredith's heart sank. "The city is too big to simply wander around and hope we run into her. Hell, we don't even know for certain this is where she came."

"True, but it makes the most sense."

"She's frightened and on the run—there's no guarantee sense is playing into any of her decisions. If she was afraid, why didn't she call you? Ask for help?"

Dominic sighed. "Good question. One I won't have the answer to until we find Tessa."

Dominic punched something into his phone, grasped her hand and started walking through the crowd. "Where are we going?"

"I figure while we wait for information or inspiration, the least we can do is check into our hotel. We're staying at the casino."

Of course they were. Why wouldn't he book a room at the biggest party location in the place? "We don't have time for gambling, Dominic." Meredith didn't even bother trying to hide the irritation in her voice.

Dominic frowned. "Of course not. But if she's being smart, the casino is the perfect place to blend in. Lie low. So that's where we'll start."

Shit. She'd jumped to conclusions again, let her past opinion of him color their current situation. When would she start realizing that wasn't a very smart thing to do where Dominic was concerned?

"I'm sorry."

"For what?"

Where did she start? "For thinking the worst of you when you've done nothing to earn that from me."

In front of her, Dominic made a soft huffing sound. "That's not entirely true, is it? I've given you plenty of reasons to think the worst of me. I've built a persona, Meredith, and embraced it a long time ago."

"But that isn't who you really are."

He shrugged but kept his focus on the people in front of them. "Isn't it?"

"No, and we both know that. So, I'm sorry."

This time, he did look back, and a soft smile tugged at the corners of his lips. "Thanks."

God, how could he make her feel any worse? His reluctant acceptance nearly slayed her. He hadn't thought twice about flying halfway around the world to help her friend who might be in danger, and not for the glory or praise. But because he genuinely wanted to help.

Meredith kept silent the rest of the way through the city. They arrived at the Hôtel de Paris and checked in. Dominic requested their bags be brought up to the room and then steered her in the direction of the casino.

It was late in the afternoon, so not exactly prime time for the glitz and glamour of Monte Carlo's repu-

tation. But the casino was clearly also a tourist destination, and all around them multiple languages could
be heard.

Not even the daylight could dim the sumptuous
decor that surrounded them. Clearly, there was a
reason people referred to Monaco as the playground
of the rich.

Together, hand in hand, they strolled through the
vast building. Meredith's gaze raced, not over the
soaring architecture and elegance that surrounded
them, but over each woman they passed. Tessa had
probably changed her hair and might have been
wearing disguising clothes, but she hoped she'd recognize the friend they were searching for.

After about an hour, Meredith could feel Dominic's frustration building. It fairly vibrated through
his body, jangling into hers through the connection
of their intertwined fingers.

"Let's take a break," she finally suggested. "My
feet are hurting and I need to change my shoes anyway."

That wasn't exactly true, but she couldn't see how
spending more time pacing past people was going to
do anyone any good.

Dominic's eyebrows pulled together in a wrinkled
frown. But he nodded and headed back in the direction of their hotel.

Their room was open and luxurious. And, Meredith noticed, unlike the suite they'd shared before,
it contained only one room. One bed.

Part of her wanted to feel irritated at his assumption. But the rest of her relished the sudden shot of need that ripped through her.

"Are you hungry?" Crossing the room, Dominic pushed his balled hands into the pockets of his pants as he stared out the windows at the gorgeous view of the waterfront spread before them.

She was beginning to realize this was a defense mechanism for him. Dominic was frustrated and probably feeling just as helpless as she was right now. Which didn't sit well with him.

Kicking off her shoes, Meredith padded across the space on silent feet. Wrapping her arms around him from behind, she pressed her body fully against his and simply waited.

Her cheek rubbed the slightly abrasive material of his suit coat. Beneath her hold, she could feel the energy trembling in his tight muscles.

Softly, she whispered, "It's going to be okay."

Meredith had no idea why she said it, but something inside her knew he needed the words. Needed to understand someone else trusted that he could solve this riddle. Protect Tessa.

And she did believe that. With everything inside her. She'd seen his determination firsthand, although something told her she still didn't fully understand it.

"Is it?" He finally asked, his own trepidation dripping from the two words.

"Yes. I have no doubt you'll use every resource at your disposal—including any you have to steal, strong-arm or borrow—to find Tessa and make sure she's safe."

"I'm glad you're certain of it, because I'm not. I've failed her already, Meredith. Obviously, I didn't protect her well enough if she felt the need to run."

Releasing her hold, Meredith slipped around to stand in front of him. Her back pressed to the cold glass even as her hand reached to the warmth of him.

"Stop that. You didn't fail her, Dominic. You saved her. You protected her. If she's in danger right now that's not your fault and certainly not from your lack of trying to keep her safe. You've done everything you can for Tessa."

Dominic's gaze searched hers before drifting above her head and back to the view of the city. "If you say so."

What the hell? Never in her life had she been so pissed at being dismissed. Grasping his cheeks, Meredith forced him to look at her. Willed him to see the truth in her words.

"You've given up a lot, and I'm not just talking about money and resources, to protect these women. Including Tessa."

"What good is that if she still gets hurt?"

The anguish in Dominic's voice, the utter despair that filled his glorious green eyes, cut straight through her.

Meredith didn't understand the strength of his reaction. Couldn't begin to combat the spiral he was clearly in if she didn't.

"Tessa isn't hurt."

"We don't know that."

"We know that she's smart enough to run when

she's afraid. And to evade even you, with all your resources. She's safe. I have to believe that."

Pressing closer, Meredith didn't stop there. "But I don't think you were talking about Tessa, were you?"

Slowly, Dominic shook his head. The soft edges of his dark mahogany hair brushed against the backs of her fingers.

It didn't take much for Meredith to make an educated guess. "Your mother?"

She'd never heard the full story, from either Dominic or Annalise. Plenty of rumors had swirled around the pair. Meredith hadn't met Annalise until several years after her mother's death, but children—especially teenagers—gossiped.

She knew that their mother had died under tragic circumstances. Meredith was smart enough to realize the sensationalized stories she'd heard couldn't all be true. But somewhere buried in the various tales of tragedy was a kernel of truth.

What really bothered her was that all the stories agreed Dominic and Annalise had been there that night. They'd seen everything.

Meredith couldn't even imagine.

Dominic's eyes squeezed shut. His entire body tensed. Balled fists slipped from his pockets and vibrated between them, almost as if he was looking for something—or someone—to punch.

But the only person in front of him was her.

Meredith waited, holding her breath, her own body poised to jump away if he lost control of the memories clearly assaulting him.

But those fists didn't search for a mark. Instead, low, graveled words started falling from his lips.

"It wasn't unusual for him to smack her around. It didn't happen every time we were there, but often enough."

A twisted laugh ripped up and out through Dominic's chest. "I didn't do anything to stop it. Until that night.

"I was ten." Which would have made Annalise eight. "And I was tired of watching it happen. That night I decided I was big enough to stand up for my mom. It was my responsibility."

A tight ball rolled through Meredith's gut. She could only guess where this was going, and it wasn't good.

"My mom had yelled at Lise and me to leave when he started, but I think we were frozen. Or at least it felt that way."

Tipping his head back, Dominic's eyes finally popped open even as he stared at the ceiling, only seeing the past.

"I don't remember everything. But I do remember grabbing his fist with both of my hands. The force of the blow as I took it instead."

Finally, he dropped his gaze, looking straight into her soul with his devastated eyes.

"I tried to protect her, but I made it worse. He didn't touch me. I wish he had. He kept screaming at me to watch what I'd caused. She ran. He grabbed her. She fell, smashing her head into a table."

God, Meredith wanted to throw up. And hold him tight.

"I think that's when the fog cleared and he realized what he'd done. He threatened both Annalise and me. He moved her to the bottom of the stairs before calling for an ambulance. Said she'd fallen."

But that wasn't how the night had gone down. "You told the truth. When the authorities arrived."

Dominic nodded. "Yes, but the investigator who arrived was a friend of my stepfather's. By the time he finished questioning me and Annalise, he'd convinced the other officers that we were both traumatized and protecting the memory of our mother. The official report was that she got drunk, lashed out at my stepfather and fell down the stairs while he was trying to calm her down."

"After all that, he came out looking like a hero."

Dominic's gaze tightened, utter fury turning his green eyes almost black. "Yes. But I made him pay. Eventually. I made sure he lost everything. It still wasn't enough."

Dominic's gaze connected with hers. The devastation there was a punch to the gut and nearly had her doubling over with the weight of his pain.

"I should have protected her. Instead I'm the reason she died."

The horror in Meredith's eyes was no less than he'd expected. The story was horrific, and the part he'd played even more so.

Turning away from her, Dominic headed for the door. He needed some air. Some distance.

He needed to shut out the expression on Meredith's face. Dammit, he'd known better than to let her matter. Not only because she deserved better than him, but because long ago he'd vowed never to give someone else the power to hurt him.

And without realizing it, sometime over their last days together, he'd handed that power to Meredith. Stupid.

He was halfway across the room when her hand on his arm stopped him.

"Where are you going?"

"Out. Away. I can't handle the way you're looking at me right now. Like I'm a monster."

"You idiot," she breathed from behind him. "You're not the monster in that story, Dominic. You're the hero."

He let out a harsh laugh. "Hardly. If you think that, then you weren't paying attention."

"Trust me, I was paying attention. Every word was like a sharp slice across my heart. No one, no kid, should have to deal with that kind of tragedy, and it hurts to know that you did. But what's worse is finally understanding that you blame yourself for what happened when you shouldn't."

Pushing on his shoulders, Meredith urged him to turn around. He could have resisted, but something inside him gave in. Part of him yearned for her to soothe the ache that had festered for so long.

"You are not responsible for your mother's death."

"Bullshit."

Her gaze was steady, her bright blue eyes glittering with determination as she said again, "You are not responsible for your mother's death. Nothing you did or said could have saved her. Nothing you did or said pushed your stepfather into some action he wasn't fully capable of on his own. I don't need to have known him to recognize that he was a violent man and eventually the same thing would have happened. But you—"

Meredith's hands gripped the side of his face, holding him steady. "You were amazing and brave. A ten-year-old boy fearless in the face of something so frightening. You protected her then, and you continue to protect her now. Every time you save some unfortunate woman headed for the same fate."

God, he wanted to believe her. To see the situation from her perspective instead of his own. But he simply couldn't.

"You weren't there. You're wrong."

"You're right. I wasn't there. But I know you. Not the man you pretend to be for the rest of the world, but the gentle, caring, loyal soul you work so damn hard to protect from more pain. And I guarantee you, if I ask Annalise, she'd agree with me. I've always known she worshipped you. Saw you as her savior and protector. I guess I understand why now. Because you were. You are."

Dominic grunted. At least on that, he could agree. "She might not see it that way. She tends to get pissy when I come between her and some guy who isn't good enough for her."

Meredith's lips curled into a smile. "Yeah, she does. But isn't that what older brothers are for? To be overly protective?"

The weight of the memories that had been spinning through his head for hours, triggered by worry over Tessa, began to ease. And he realized for the first time that the most gorgeous woman he'd ever laid eyes on was standing in front of him, the gentle touch of her palms cupping his cheeks.

The expression in her eyes wasn't one of loathing—it was one of…appreciation and pride.

Which also scared the hell out of him.

Rather than deal with the jumbled-up emotions those thoughts caused, Dominic decided to take advantage of the situation. Bending his head, he snagged her mouth with his and dived into the solace of her kiss.

Meredith responded immediately. Her fingers curled into his skin, gripping tighter and pulling him closer.

Heat spun between them, quickly burning through anything but the need they created in each other.

Scooping her off her feet, Dominic cradled her against his body as he strode toward the single open doorway and the massive bed waiting behind it.

Fourteen

"Good morning," Meredith's sleepy voice greeted him. Turning, Dominic simply took her in.

She stood, framed by the doorway of the bedroom, rumpled, flushed and sexy as hell. She'd grabbed his shirt and tugged it on. It was huge on her, the neckline hanging halfway down to reveal the curve of one naked shoulder. The hem barely skimmed the tops of her thighs, and Dominic seriously wondered if she'd bothered putting anything on underneath it.

Her hair was a cloud of red-gold piled high into a messy knot. Strands stuck out wildly, and honestly, it was the most disheveled he'd ever seen her. And she looked glorious.

"Hi."

"What are you doing out here?"

Dominic shrugged. He'd been tempted to stay in bed with her, his own body curled tight around hers as she slept. But because he'd wanted it so much, he'd forced himself to get up.

"I don't sleep much. I didn't want to disturb you."

Behind him, the sky was just finally turning pale blue as the last fingers of dawn let go to welcome the day.

Meredith eyed him. "I wouldn't have minded."

Honestly, the truth was he'd woken up feeling raw, exposed and a little unnerved at all he'd shared with her the night before. And he hadn't been ready to face it just yet. But he wasn't ready to tell her that, either.

"No reason we both needed to be awake."

Reaching both arms over her head, Meredith grasped the top of the door frame. Rising on her tip-toes, she stretched. His shirt climbed several inches up her thighs, revealing that she had, in fact, not bothered to put on anything beneath.

His physical response was instantaneous. A full-on erection slammed into the unyielding line of his zipper, making Dominic draw in a hiss of breath at the pleasure-pain.

God, he wanted her. Again. Never in his life had he felt this driving need to take, possess, consume. But it was more than sex with Meredith. He'd experienced strong physical connections before in his life.

He wanted her approval, which was uncharted territory for him. He wanted more. If he was being honest, he wanted everything. He wanted her to love him, which left him feeling utterly exposed.

And he wasn't ready to deal with that just yet, either.

So, instead, he chose the easy path. The one he was comfortable and familiar with. Crossing the room, he grasped the hem of his shirt and used it to tug her against him.

His mouth to the delicate skin at her neck, he growled, "I don't remember saying you could borrow my clothes."

Meredith laughed, the soft sound floating between them. "What are you going to do about it?"

"Take it back."

"Is that right?" Twisting out of his hold, Meredith darted back inside the bedroom, tossing over her shoulder, "You can try."

He loved seeing her this way. Carefree and playful. So unlike the woman he'd always known. It felt like she was sharing a secret with him, showing him pieces of herself that she kept hidden from everyone else.

Which went a long way to soothing his own jangled nerves at ripping open his own secret places.

They came together in a blaze of heat. Laughter, moans, grasping fingers and soul-deep sighs. For some reason, Dominic wanted to prolong the experience, to etch the feel and taste of her deep into his memory.

When they finally tipped over, it was together.

Her orgasm bleeding into his own. Her cries of pleasure echoing out with his.

Together, they collapsed onto the bed, a tangle of limbs and sweat-slicked skin.

Finally, Meredith pushed up onto one elbow and grinned down at him. "If this was what you had planned for the morning, you could have woken me up anytime."

Dominic couldn't stop his own grin from responding to hers. "I'll remember that."

"As much as I hate to ruin the mood by bringing reality back into it, what's the plan for today?"

Dominic rolled onto his back. That was the other reason he'd been awake so early. Frustration, guilt and a drowning sense of helplessness rode him hard. "I honestly have no idea." Rolling his head to look at her, he said, "I'm open to suggestions."

Meredith's lips pursed into a frown. "I really wish we knew for certain we were in the right place. I mean, it's possible she did come here but didn't stay. She could have hopped another train immediately."

That was true, but they'd shown Tessa's picture to several of the train station attendants when they'd arrived, and no one had recognized her. While that might be possible if she was just another tourist getting off the train, it would have been more difficult to stay completely unseen if she'd interacted with employees to buy a ticket and load onto another train.

No, Dominic's gut told him the key to finding Tessa was here. And until something else proved his gut wrong...

He was about to voice that very thought when Meredith's cell phone on the bedside table trilled loudly.

Reaching for it, Dominic was momentarily distracted by the expanse of her belly and hip as she arched beneath him. Licking his tongue across his lips, he started to lean forward so he could snag a taste of her. Meredith's eyes danced with joy and laughter as she put a palm to his face, stopping him with a slow shake of her head.

She didn't even bother looking at the screen before answering the call. "Hello?"

That joy melted away as she jackknifed up in the bed. "Yeah, he's right here."

Holding the phone out to him, she said, "It's Joker. You weren't answering your phone, so he called mine. I'd ask how he knows my number, but that would be a stupid question."

She was right. It would be a stupid question. Grabbing the phone, Dominic said, "Talk to me."

"She called in."

This time, it was Dominic's turn to sit straight up. But he didn't stay there long. Leaping from the bed, he switched the phone to his other ear even as he searched the floor for clothes he could throw on.

"Where is she? Why'd she run? Is she safe?"

"Slow down, man." Joker's voice was hard, but without panic or urgency. "She's fine. For now. She called in from a burner."

"Good girl."

"Yeah, she listened when we told her how to stay

safe. Originally, she didn't call because she was afraid that whoever was tailing her was somehow attached to the team or that the team had been compromised. But she realized that she was quickly running out of cash and had to risk asking for help."

Thank God for small favors.

"Where is she?" Dominic wanted all the questions answered, but right now, that was the most important one. They could sort everything else out once Tessa was safe.

"You were right. She's in Monaco."

"I'm going with you." In Meredith's mind, that wasn't even a question.

"No, I'm going alone. Tessa knows me. Trusts me. She might get spooked if she sees anyone else."

Meredith simply raised an eyebrow. "I've known Tessa longer than you have."

"Maybe, but she didn't trust you with what was happening."

The arrow hit, although she seriously hoped it hadn't been an intentional one. Dominic was clearly not only in a hurry, but in savior mode. Which was a role she was coming to realize he filled very often.

And thanks to their conversation last night, now she better understood why, which also helped mitigate her own irritation at his stonewalling her.

Suddenly realizing what he'd just done, Dominic stopped in his tracks, closed his eyes and let out a sigh. Crossing the room, he grasped her hands and pulled her close.

"I'm sorry. I didn't mean that the way it came out."

Meredith simply nodded, silently accepting his apology.

"If Tessa is being followed, is in danger, the less conspicuous we are, the better for her. There's a reason we don't go storming in and remove these women by force. They're safer with fewer people who know what's happening."

"I already know what's happening."

His fingers squeezed hers. "I know. But I'd feel better keeping with protocol and only sending one person in. Alone, I'm likely to garner less attention."

It wasn't as if she dressed like a flamboyant peacock or had neon-blue hair. But she could see this was important to him, for whatever reason. And while Tessa was her friend, this was his area of expertise.

"Fine." If he wanted to go alone, she'd let him.

"Thank you," he said, leaning down to give her a soft, easy kiss. "It would be a huge help if you packed everything up so we could leave as soon as she's secured."

Great. Relegated to luggage duty. "Whatever," she grumbled. Dominic's mouth quirked up into a smile. Not the practiced, calculated, charming smile he used on everyone else. His real smile. The one she'd begun to see more and more often.

Meredith's heart squeezed tight. Whatever she had to do in order to be on the receiving end of that smile was totally worth it. Even packing.

She watched him grab his cell, wallet and room

key and race out the door. As soon as he was gone, she realized he hadn't even told her where he was going. Or when he'd be back.

With a shrug, Meredith realized it probably didn't matter. Strolling into the bedroom, she began gathering their things.

Somehow it felt even more intimate to be folding his clothes and placing them in his duffel than it had been to tear them off his body just hours before. The buzz of memory wasn't really helping the situation, either.

Meredith had no idea how long she'd been in the bedroom, maybe twenty or thirty minutes. She'd been prolonging the task, knowing that once it was finished there wasn't much left to do except sit and wait. But it wasn't long before the doorknob rattled.

Throwing the last couple things into her own bag, Meredith headed for the door to their suite, "Well, that didn't take long," already on her lips.

But the words died as she stared at the strange man standing just inside the room.

"Who are you?"

Dominic knocked on the door to the third-rate hotel room. This was the place Joker had told him Tessa was staying, and looking around, he wanted to hurt someone.

Monte Carlo was gorgeous and affluent, but that didn't mean there wasn't still a seedy side to the city. And apparently, Tessa had found it.

The door creaked open, and a single eyeball

greeted him. He waited, careful not to move or push inside until Tessa felt safe enough to open the door.

With a hiccuping sob, she did just that, jerking the barrier out of the way and falling into his arms as he crossed the threshold.

"Thank God you were close" was all she said before burying her face in his chest. Tears quickly soaked the front of his shirt, but he didn't particularly care. Clearly, Tessa had been scared out of her mind.

Dominic let her cry, shifting them into the room and over to the single bed that occupied the dingy space. The cheap material of the spread slid against the mattress, making a slithering sound that jangled against his nerves.

When her crying jag began to slow, Dominic finally started asking questions.

"Why are you here, Tessa? What happened?"

Sniffling, she pulled away. Using the back of her hand, she wiped at the tracks of tears down her cheeks. Gone was the woman he'd first met with her blond extensions, fake eyelashes and talon nails. Her expensive designer bag and shoes and clothes.

Tessa had dyed her platinum blond to a rich caramel brown. She'd pulled the shorter strands back into a stubby ponytail at the base of her skull, and her face was completely free of makeup. Before, she'd looked artificial and miserable. Today, despite the tears, she looked fresh and a hell of a lot happier.

"Someone was following me."

"You're sure?"

She nodded. "Yeah, I was watching, using the

techniques you guys taught me. At first, I just chalked up the creepy-crawly sensation at the back of my neck to being paranoid. But then I kept seeing this guy. Wherever I went, he was there. And he looked mean."

There was no question in Dominic's mind that Tessa believed the man had been following her.

"One night, walking home from getting dinner, I turned the corner a couple blocks away from home, and he was just there. Lurking in the shadows. I ran back to the restaurant I'd been at and asked for help."

Thank God someone had been there for her.

"He followed me inside. I ran out the back, grabbed my stuff and left."

Dominic rubbed a soothing hand down her arm.

"You didn't recognize him?"

"No, which scared me even more."

Shaking his head, Dominic said, "I bet it did. Do you think you could describe him?"

Nodding, Tessa reached behind her for a notebook on the bedside table. "I can do more than that. I've got a sketch."

Dominic's eyebrows rose as she handed him a black-and-gray pencil drawing. The man's face was detailed and clear.

Clear enough for Dominic to identify him immediately.

Rage twisted through Dominic's gut, but he grasped the reins and pulled it back. The last thing Tessa needed to see right now was a display of temper.

That kind of thing had already scarred her enough.

Rising, Dominic gently pointed her in the direction of her bag. "I'm going outside to make a couple calls. Come outside when you're ready."

Tessa's hand gripped his for several seconds, but after a moment, she let go.

Dominic was careful not to slam the door behind him, even though he really wanted to. But the minute the barrier was closed, he hit speed dial straight to Joker.

He didn't even bother with niceties, just launched into "We have a major problem. I know who's been following Tessa."

Fifteen

Dominic paused at the hotel room door. He'd been so intent on getting back to Meredith that he hadn't stopped to think that Tessa wasn't even aware her friend was there.

"There's someone inside that I hope you'll be happy to see."

Tessa's eyebrows scrunched down in confusion. "What?"

"Meredith came with me."

Her mouth opened but then closed without voicing any of the questions he could see behind her eyes. "Okay," she finally said.

Letting it go at that, Dominic opened the door wide and ushered Tessa inside. His gaze scanned the room, expecting to see Meredith waiting for them on the sofa. She wasn't there.

Walking to the bedroom doorway, he called, "Meredith?"

But there was no answer. The shower wasn't running in the bathroom. She wasn't in the room.

Nerves spun through his belly. Dominic tamped them down. Surely there was a logical explanation. Maybe she'd run out to get something to eat? Although that didn't sound like Meredith. She'd known what he was doing and would have waited.

"Dominic?" Tessa's voice trembled, making the bottom drop out of his stomach.

Stalking across the room, he stared down at the remnants of the house phone lying in pieces. Fear and regret stormed through him, a sick sludge that threatened to completely take over.

He'd left her alone. He'd left her vulnerable. Put her in danger and then couldn't protect her.

"Dominic?" Tessa's voice and the soft hand on his arm jolted him.

He needed to find Meredith. Now.

Grabbing his cell, he punched a number straight to Joker. "Meredith's been taken."

"What?" From the other end of the line, Joker sounded distracted. He needed his friend's full attention.

"Stop what you're doing and listen to me. We got back to the room and Meredith is gone. The phone is smashed into bits on the floor."

A silent pause whispered down the line before the

furious tapping of fingers on keys broke through. "I'm hacking into the hotel's security feeds right now. You think it's Michael?"

Dominic closed his eyes. "That's my guess. Find her."

He didn't want to think about what that psycho could be doing to Meredith. Michael was the ex of Amanda, a woman they helped almost two years ago. From what he knew of the man, if Michael ever connected Dominic to his ex-wife's disappearance, he was definitely the type to seek revenge. Before being hidden Amanda had told him Michael was a narcissistic psychopath with no compunctions about hurting anyone who stood in his way.

At first, Stone had kept him under surveillance, but when months went by while Michael lived his life like he never had a wife, let alone like she'd been reported missing, they'd dropped it.

Apparently, too soon. Because from Tessa's drawing, Dominic had no doubt that's who had been stalking her. Why he was stalking Tessa was another question, but no doubt it had something to do with finding Amanda.

Meredith wasn't going to be able to help him with that. But surely Michael would figure that out. Would he use her as leverage against Dominic for information?

Dominic wanted to smash his fist into the wall in front of him. Faced with a choice between protecting Meredith and protecting Amanda, whom would he choose?

No, there was no question. He'd pick Meredith. Not just because she was damned important to him—and until this moment, he hadn't realized just how much. But because they could get to Amanda before Michael could. In fact, Stone was already in the process of contacting her and getting her moved to a new location.

Spinning in a circle, Dominic searched the room for anything that might help him out. Point him in the direction of where Meredith might be.

But there was nothing. Not even a piece of torn clothing or a button.

Reaching up, he threaded his fingers through his hair and pulled. He couldn't just sit here and wait.

Giving Tessa instructions to throw the bolt in the door behind him and not let anyone but him or Meredith inside, Dominic headed for the door.

Tessa's chin trembled, but she nodded.

Dominic barreled into the hallway, pausing long enough to listen as Tessa threw the bolt into place. Striding for the elevator, he scanned the carpet in every direction. Searching for…something.

Hitting the button to call the elevator car, Dominic tapped his foot impatiently. It dinged its arrival, the doors sliding open. Down the hall, another door opened, the sound of the click echoing through the quiet space.

Dominic turned, half in and half out of the elevator, to watch a bruised and bloody Meredith stumble into the hallway.

Sixteen

Sluggish and uncoordinated, Meredith's body wasn't responding to the instructions from her brain.

But she needed to keep moving. Get away.

Michael, the man who'd barged into her hotel room, had forced her out and down the hallway to another room. She knew it was a bad idea to go with him, but he'd given her no choice.

He'd tied her to a chair and, in between blows, had ranted at her about Dominic, someone named Amanda and the fact that she hadn't published the story like he'd wanted.

Two things were clear, the man was unhinged, and he was the source of the anonymous email she'd received.

Luckily, he'd made a mistake, letting his anger

overrule his awareness, and Meredith had taken advantage, escaping.

Meredith might have knocked him out, but that could only last a few moments. She needed those precious seconds to find help.

"Meredith." From down the hall, she heard Dominic's voice. The single word went in and out, like someone was playing with the volume inside her ears.

Her hand trembled, palm flat against the wall as she fought to stay upright. The world spun. Her gaze jerked up to see the blur of him sprinting toward her.

Instinct had her flinching away when he grabbed for her. But the second his hands wrapped around her, hauling her against the solid surface of his body, Meredith let out a whimpering sob. She was safe.

"Dominic." She let him take her weight. But, no, they couldn't just stand here. As much as she wanted to bask in the protection and comfort he was offering.

"We need to get downstairs. Call security. Get help."

"On it, angel," he murmured, sliding a soft hand down the length of her hair. Gathering her up, Dominic guided her back to their room. Knocking, he identified himself before the bolt moved and the door swung open to reveal Tessa on the other side.

A smile broke across Meredith's face. She didn't even care that it pulled at the jagged edge of the cut in the corner. "It's really good to see you."

Tessa frowned. "You look like hell."

"Gee, thanks."

Behind them, Dominic was talking to someone, probably the front desk, explaining what had happened.

Over the next several hours, Meredith gave her statement to security, to the local police and then again to the medical team that showed up to treat her.

They tried to insist she be taken to the hospital, but Meredith refused. Not even Dominic's growling anger or dangerous green eyes could convince her.

Her body ached, but she knew there was nothing they could do for her that time wouldn't accomplish. A few cuts and bruises. Possibly a mild concussion, although the ringing in her ears and blurry vision had already cleared.

At one point, she heard someone tell Dominic that Michael had been taken into custody.

That should have given her a sense of peace. And maybe in some small part of her mind, it did.

But from the moment the authorities had arrived, Dominic had barely spoken to her—except to argue when she refused to go to the hospital. He definitely hadn't touched her. He was back to the aloof, disinterested man she'd always known.

And that scared the hell out of her. More than Michael even had.

The boulder in the pit of her stomach said something was off. But each time she tried to get close to Dominic so they could talk, he found a reason to shut her off. Shut her out.

Hell, he'd barely even looked at her. And when he did, those glorious green eyes were…distant.

What she really wanted was for everyone else to just disappear. For Dominic to wrap his arms around her and hold her tight.

Instead, Tessa was the one sitting beside her. Gripping her hand as she went through the details of what had happened for what felt like a hundred times.

And when they finally got onto the private plane waiting at the airport for them, nothing much changed. Dominic found a reason to sit as far away as he could. "I'm going to be handling some calls for work and don't want to disturb you. Get some rest."

Yeah, right. By the time they landed in Vegas, Meredith was a bundle of nerves.

Gathering her stuff, she stood in the aisle, waiting for Dominic to meet her. He'd have to walk past her eventually, unless he wanted to camp out on the plane. And she could be just as stubborn as he was.

But when he saw her waiting, Dominic didn't even hesitate. Leaning around her, he spoke to Tessa, "There's a car waiting outside. The driver has your itinerary and everything you need to start again. I'm so sorry you got caught up in this mess. But know it had nothing to do with you. You're safe."

"Thanks," Tessa said, nodding. Grasping Meredith's hand, her friend squeezed. "You'll be okay?"

"Yeah, I'm fine. Nothing a little time won't heal." Squeezing her hand back, Meredith continued, "Good luck. When you feel it's safe, let me know where you are. I'm sorry I wasn't there for you when you needed a friend."

With a wave, Tessa disappeared down the stairs. Meredith heard her greet the guy at the bottom waiting for her and the roar of the engine as her car pulled away.

Turning back, Meredith waited for Dominic to say something. Anything.

He watched her, his eyes flat and dark. She desperately wanted to see that spark, the mischief and irritation. Anything other than the blank stare of someone looking straight through her.

Finally, he said, "Your driver is waiting."

"My driver?"

"He'll take you home."

Meredith tipped her head sideways. "I thought we'd go home together." The throb that had eased right between her eyes began again.

Taking a step toward her, Dominic reached out a hand, but he let it drop before he actually touched her. "Look, you know who I am. I don't do this." Dominic waved a finger between the two of them. "We have chemistry, I won't deny that. But Paris was easy. I've always wondered what you'd be like in bed, and now I know. It's time for both of us to go back to our lives. You want something I'll never be able to give you."

Meredith felt like she'd been punched in the gut. Again. But she refused to let him see the pain his words inflicted. Tears burned the backs of her eyes, but she blinked them away.

Hadn't she always known this was where they were headed? Why she'd kept her distance from

Dominic for all those years? Yes, he was sexy as hell. And over the last weeks, she'd learned he was a lot more complex than she'd ever given him credit for.

But at his core, he was selfish, only caring about his own pleasure and convenience.

Meredith forced words through her raw throat, "As you wish," before turning around and walking off the plane.

Every bone in her body urged her to turn back. To fight for him. But that wouldn't get her anywhere. And she had too much pride to try and convince Dominic they had something worth exploring.

If he didn't want her, she didn't want him.

But, God, it hurt. More than Michael's punches. More than her bruised ribs and split lip. The wounds Dominic had inflicted went so much deeper.

Climbing into the car, Meredith refused to look behind her. But she did tell the driver, "Take me to the Magnifique."

Annalise might ask questions she wasn't ready for, but that was better than being alone. Right now, she couldn't handle that.

Dominic wanted to break something. Watching Meredith walk away from him had ripped his guts out.

But the wounded light in her eyes, the cuts and bruises across her body…they'd been reminders that she was better off without him.

He hadn't kept her safe. But worse than that, he'd

actively put her in the line of fire. She'd paid the price for the decisions he'd made. Just like his mother.

He'd almost lost her. After speaking with the investigators, Dominic had no doubts Michael would have gleefully killed Meredith. The man had no conscience, and if he'd thought it would get him one step closer to finding his wife, he'd have done it.

Dominic lived in a dangerous world. And not simply because of the women he helped. He lived his entire life in the shadows. Thrived in the dark, seedy underside of the night. Sure, he did everything he could to keep drugs out of his club, to ensure the people who partied with him were as safe as possible. But he lived in Vegas where excess and bad decisions went hand in hand.

Taking risks for himself, that was easy. Putting Meredith in the same line of fire...not acceptable.

She was better off without him, not wrapped up in his world. They'd only been together for a few days, really. It was better this way. Better that he break things off now. Before either of them got in too deep.

Dominic rubbed at the center of his chest, trying to will away the ache where his heart should have been. It wasn't there. Meredith had taken it with her when she'd left.

Staring out at the party on the dance floor of Excess, Dominic knew he should be out there. Touching base with his staff. Checking on his business. Making sure things had operated smoothly in his absence.

Later. He'd deal with that later. Right now, he needed to be alone.

Hell, he hadn't even flipped the lights on in his office. He wasn't ready for anyone to know he was back.

Reaching down, he grabbed the cut crystal tumbler he'd filled almost to the top with single-malt scotch. Knocking it back, he let the fire burn down his throat and into his belly.

That would take the pain away. At least for a little while.

The door opened and closed behind him with a quiet click. Dominic fought the urge to bellow at whoever had disturbed his peace. Only one person knew he was here, and he was waiting for a report. Not good management to jump down the throat of the person giving you the info you'd asked for.

Jake sauntered up to stand beside him. Dropping his hands into his own pockets, the other man mirrored Dominic's stance. He stood there, silent, for several seconds.

Dominic's nerves stretched taut, and he finally snapped, "Well?"

Jake glanced at him, assessing, before returning his gaze to the club. "Tessa is on the plane. They'll make several stops, but she'll arrive at her final destination tomorrow afternoon."

They'd added a couple of extra layers of twists and turns to her hop to her new home. Just in case.

"Let me know when she arrives."

Jake nodded. "I will."

Having delivered his message, Dominic expected

Jake to leave. Instead, he hung around, quietly invading Dominic's brooding.

Finally, when he couldn't take any more, Dominic turned. "Is there something else?" Even he could hear the cold, irritated tone in his own voice. He knew it was uncalled for but couldn't stop it. Jake was a convenient outlet.

"I thought you might like to know that Meredith didn't go home."

That got his full attention. "What?"

"She redirected her driver to Magnifique."

Annalise. She'd gone to see her best friend. It might be late, but Lise worked the same strange hours he did, so she would be up. Dominic still didn't want Annalise involved, and he'd prefer she not know the truth. But after the experience she'd had, Meredith needed someone. That couldn't be him, so he wouldn't stop her from seeking out her best friend.

Turning back to the spectacle below, Dominic said, "She can go wherever she wants."

Jake rocked back on his heels. "True. But I thought you might like to know where she was…in case you pulled your head out of your ass and decided to go after her. That woman is one in a million and worth holding on to."

Rage blasted through Dominic. "Stay away from her," he growled.

Jake laughed. "Man, I'm not stupid. We've been friends for a long time, and I have no desire to get on your bad side by going after the woman you love."

"I don't love her."

"Bullshit. Lie to everyone else, but don't lie to yourself. I've watched you with a ton of women over the years. She's different."

Jake's hand landed on his shoulder, his fingers tightening. "Here's some unsolicited advice. I don't know what stupid thing you did, but I suggest you figure out how to undo it and go after her. Before someone else scoops her up."

Without waiting for an answer, Jake strode out the door. Dominic's mind spun.

Did he love her?

Maybe.

No, there was no maybe about it. He loved Meredith, and some part of him had always known that if he let himself get close to her, this was exactly what would happen. That's why he'd kept his distance all that time.

The real question was, did loving her change anything?

The memory of watching Meredith stumble from that room, bloody and bruised, blasted through his mind. He'd never forget that moment. The paralyzing fear, helplessness and guilt.

Because he'd felt them before. And vowed he'd never feel them again.

So, no, it didn't matter. At the end of the day, Meredith couldn't love him. He'd failed her, just as he'd failed his mom. She'd never be able to look at him and not be reminded of the pain and fear he'd dragged her into.

* * *

Meredith walked into Annalise's office at Magnifique. It wasn't the first time she'd been there. Heck, it wasn't even the hundredth.

But the last time, she'd come to ask for help in questioning Dominic's integrity and humanity.

Now, she had no question about those things. Dominic was a good man, and not even the way he'd brushed her off and ended their…affair could change her mind on that. She'd seen it with her own eyes, the man he tried to hide and protect.

Which was maybe why she hurt so much. She knew he had it in him to be a better person. To treat her better than he had.

He simply chose not to.

Annalise looked up from the computer screen she'd been staring at. Her eyes squinted and there were lines drawn on either side of her mouth, like the frown she was wearing had been etched into her skin.

Her friend was too damn young for that kind of thing.

"What's wrong?" Meredith asked.

"What?" Annalise blinked at her, clearing away the expression. "Oh, nothing. I'm just going over some numbers and trying to understand why they're off. I'll figure it out."

Of that, Meredith had no doubt. Her friend was not only a good businesswoman, but she was a bulldog once she had a bone. And she hated disorder. If there was something off on the report, she'd track it down.

"But right now, I'm more interested in why your eyes are puffy and red-rimmed. Who's the asshole I need to kill for making you cry?"

Meredith had held it together getting off the plane, but once inside the car, she hadn't been able to hold back the pain and grief. Part of her hated herself for the weakness, but the rest of her realized that Dominic had hurt her. And the reaction was normal.

Plopping down onto the sofa on the far side of the room, Meredith dropped her head onto the back. She rubbed the heels of her palms into her gritty eyes.

"Come on. Spill," Annalise urged. The opposite end of the couch compressed beneath the weight as her friend joined her.

Dropping her hands, Meredith stared at the ceiling. It was easier than looking at Annalise as she confessed, "Your brother."

Meredith wasn't sure what she'd expected, but the silent nothing from her friend wasn't it. Maybe anger at Dominic. Or irritation at Meredith for being stupid and dipping her toes into that water.

Both reactions were valid.

But the quiet…

Meredith finally rolled her head to look at Annalise.

The soft smile curling her friend's mouth definitely hadn't entered onto the list of possible reactions.

"What are you smiling about?"

"I'm happy you two finally stopped fighting it

and gave in to what's been between you for years. Did you honestly think I wasn't aware?"

"Did you miss the part where I've been crying for the past twenty minutes because he broke my heart?"

Annalise reached out and placed a comforting hand on Meredith's arm. "I'm sorry. I know it sucks. But I have faith that whatever stupid thing my brother's done can be overcome."

"Maybe it was me, not him."

Lise raised an eyebrow. "We both know out of you guys, he's the one most likely to sabotage a good thing. Now, tell me what happened."

Meredith spent the next twenty minutes filling her friend in on the whirlwind trip through Europe. Annalise didn't even blink when she mentioned Tessa. Her only response was to say, "Glad she's out of that terrible situation."

Her soft smile returned when Meredith mentioned that Dominic had opened up and shared details about what had happened with their mother. At another time, Meredith would have taken the time to express her own sorrow for what they'd both gone through and the mother they'd lost. But she was too wrapped up in her own pain right now.

Annalise's mouth tightened and those frown lines reappeared as Meredith explained the scene with Michael.

"That explains the bruises and cuts. I knew Dominic hadn't given them to you."

Meredith shook her head. "He couldn't. Wouldn't."

"Exactly."

When the story was all said and done, Meredith felt…lost. Alone in a way that she never had, despite the fact that she'd been on her own for almost ten years.

"You love him." Annalise's words jerked Meredith's gaze to hers.

She opened her mouth to refute the statement. No, she didn't love him. They'd only had a few days together, right?

Although she had known him for a huge chunk of her life. And during that time, he'd been an irritation more than anything. Sure, a sexy, handsome one, but there was more to love than physical attraction.

The ache in the center of her chest was what kept her from making the denial. Because even though they'd only been together for a few days, walking away from him hurt. She hadn't thought about a future or built a house with a picket fence in her head. But that didn't mean the idea of potential hadn't always been there.

Hell, wasn't that what had irritated her most about him over all those years? She *knew* the man he could be.

Meredith shook her head. The man he already was.

"Yes," she finally whispered.

Annalise squealed, lurching forward as she wrapped her arms around Meredith and pulled her in tight. "I'm so happy for you both."

Her friend's reaction was bewildering. "I love him. He obviously doesn't love me. He told me what we had was nothing. Easy. And over. Did you forget that?"

Annalise waved her hand in front of her face, as if the gesture could wipe Meredith's words out of existence.

"Bullshit. Don't you get it? You scare him. There's a reason no woman has ever been in his life long-term. He doesn't trust himself to let anyone close. He's afraid of losing someone who matters to him again."

It was a good interpretation. "When did you get your psych degree?"

"Don't need one. I've been through plenty of therapy myself, and I understand my brother. He has a noble streak a mile wide, although he prefers to hide it."

Well, that was certainly true. Meredith had seen evidence of it firsthand.

"What happened to you with Michael was his worst fear come to life, Meredith. He cares for you, and you were hurt. My guess is he's blaming himself right about now. And figured pushing you away was the best way to protect you. And himself."

Meredith let Annalise's words spin through her head. She weighed them. Studied them. Tried to poke holes in what her friend was saying...but when she really looked at it, it made sense.

From the moment he'd known she was safe, Dominic had begun to pull away. She'd seen the utter horror in his eyes when she'd looked up to find him standing in the hallway.

She'd been too preoccupied with the relief flooding through her to really catalog and analyze it then. She'd simply assumed his reaction was because she was battered and bloodied. Could Annalise be right? Could it have been more?

"I hadn't thought about it that way."

Annalise's mouth twisted into a sad smile. "Why would you? You didn't go through what he and I experienced."

Hope bloomed inside Meredith's chest, slowly pushing against the despair that had flooded her when Dominic told her to go.

"But that doesn't mean he loves me. We've only been together a few days."

"What does that matter? You've known each other for a long time. And I've always known the irritation you both sparked off each other was just a cover for the stronger emotions neither of you wanted to admit to. You were both protecting yourselves. But Dominic isn't doing that anymore."

Meredith laughed, the sound scraping through her throat. "Oh yeah? What do you call sending me away?"

"I call that the last gasps of a man's dying denial. Meredith, he trusted you enough to talk about our mother. He shared the worst moment in his life, what *he* deems the worst thing he's ever done. He doesn't talk about that night with anyone, including me. And I was there with him. He wouldn't share that with you if he didn't love you."

Meredith's throat closed. The tears she'd thought were spent burned at the back of her eyes.

Placing her arms around Meredith, Annalise pulled her into a comforting embrace. "Where's the tenacious woman I know and love? You take life by storm, Meredith, and always have. Most people are afraid of Dominic, but you never have been. You've been calling him on his shit since he was fifteen. Why aren't you doing it tonight? Take a breath and then go find my brother and tell him what an ass he's being. Tell him that you love him. Tell him he's a good man. And then don't leave until he admits that you matter and he needs you in his life."

Meredith laughed, the sound wheezing out of her tight chest. "You make it sound so easy."

Pulling back, Annalise's sharp expression eased. "Of course it isn't. Nothing worth having in this life is. But trust me, I know firsthand that life can be short and you never know what curveball is headed your way. Don't let pride or fear stop you from having something you want."

God, Annalise was right. What the hell was Meredith doing at Magnifique when she should be storming the office at Excess?

Seventeen

A loud bang ricocheted through the office as the door bounced against the wall.

"Asshole." The single word echoed around the room right behind the announcement from the swinging door.

Meredith marched into the office, not bothering to close the door behind her. Not that anyone else was in the executive suite at this time of night, anyway. Jake was following up with Stone on Tessa's progress, and the rest of his security team were making sweeps through the club in preparation for last call and closing in an hour.

Fire shot through Meredith's bright blue eyes. Joy bubbled through his blood…until he cut it off. No, he couldn't be happy to see her. And, clearly, Meredith wasn't happy to see him, if the irritation rolling off her was any indication.

Crossing his arms, Dominic spread his feet wide, as if preparing for a physical punch.

If he was honest, he'd expected this confrontation at some point. Meredith wasn't the type of woman to take the rejection he'd given her without a fight. He'd expected to have a day or two to prepare, though.

For his own emotions to be less raw.

No matter. He'd give her whatever she needed in order to move on with her life. To find something better for her than he could ever be.

"I'm not sure I deserve the label, but whatever. What can I do for you, Meredith? I thought I was clear earlier that we didn't have anything else to talk about."

Meredith stalked across the room, her feet slapping the floor with each step. "Oh, you were clear about a few things, but now it's my turn."

Stopping inches from him, she grasped his shoulders, jerked him into her and set her mouth against his. The kiss was brutal and bruising. Filled with exasperation, but beneath that was the burning heat that was always there when they touched. A complexity of emotions, wants, needs.

And the soft spring taste of hope.

Jerking back, she whispered, "I love you, you idiot."

Dominic blinked. His ears buzzed, making him pretty sure that he'd heard her wrong. "What?"

The harsh emotions filling her gaze melted away.

Her hold on him softened. Her hands drifted up his shoulders to cup his face. "I love you," she murmured, staring straight into his soul.

Dominic's throat closed, and his stomach rolled. Not with joy, but a sickly sludge of emotions. Fear, hope, guilt.

"No, you don't." He shook his head. "You shouldn't. I don't deserve your love."

Meredith's lips trembled, and a sheen of tears shimmered at the edge of her lashes. "Too bad, because I do. And I'll argue until I'm blue in the face that you deserve my love, and the love of everyone else in your life who cares about you. You're a good man, Dominic. Strong, protective. Worthy."

"I'm not."

Meredith shook her head. "You are."

"You were hurt, Meredith. Because of a decision *I* made. Because of something *I* did." The words stuck in his throat, but he forced them out on a ragged whisper— "Just like my mom."

"I wasn't hurt because of something you did. I was hurt because a madman exists in the world. A madman you were trying to protect someone from. Your mother wasn't killed because you did or said something. She was killed because she married someone with a darkness inside that he couldn't control. Your stepfather would have killed your mother eventually, that night or another. And nothing you could have done or said would have stopped him. Or made him do anything."

Pain twisted through Dominic's chest. He tried

to push out of Meredith's grasp, but her fingers tightened and she wouldn't let him go. Instead, she brought her face close and looked him straight in the eye.

"I see you, Dominic. The man you truly are. You spend your life protecting the people you care about. You spend your life protecting complete strangers. You have a good soul and you deserve happiness. Now, if you want to tell me that you don't love me, I'll walk out that door and never see you again. But as long as your reason for pushing me away is because you don't think you deserve me… I'm not going anywhere."

Dominic stared into Meredith's eyes. He looked deep and saw a reflection of his own staring back. Hopeful, devastated, afraid.

He wanted to tell her that he didn't love her, but the words wouldn't come. Because they weren't true.

Meredith was everything he'd ever wanted in his life. She was good and kind. Strong and demanding. She could be opinionated and annoying as hell when she didn't agree with him…but that was okay. He'd rather have a woman in his life who would stand up to him and tell him when he was being an ass than a doormat who was afraid of her shadow.

He needed someone strong by his side. Someone he wouldn't have to fear would disappear beneath the weight of his own strong personality.

Meredith was perfect for him and always had been.

"I'm pretty sure I've loved you since the night I first kissed you and then you told me to pound sand."

A slow smile bloomed across Meredith's face. It lit her eyes from the inside, joy radiating out of her and making her glow. While he loved riling her up and the fire that shot out of her when he triggered her temper, the elation of watching her bloom under the weight of his love was ten times better.

So he said it again. "Meredith Forrester, I love you."

Making a whooping sound that was completely unexpected, she jumped into his arms, wrapping her legs around his waist as she clung to him.

Her mouth rained kisses across his face before finding his lips. The kiss was deep, and yes, his body responded. But there was more than physical reaction.

Happiness bloomed to life, spreading warmth through his entire body. He held her tight. They might not have it all figured out, but they'd get there.

For now, all he needed to know was she was his.

Epilogue

Annalise watched the couple across the room, a small grin curling her lips. It was so good to see her brother and best friend happy.

Dominic and Meredith had been together for a couple of months, and to no one's surprise, this party was being thrown to announce their engagement.

She'd always known that once Dominic got his head out of his ass, it wouldn't take him long to want to get Meredith wrapped up tight and tied to him in every way he possibly could.

Being happy for them was easy. They both deserved it. And Annalise had to admit, it didn't suck that her best friend was going to become her sister. She'd always thought of Meredith that way anyway.

Since Dominic ran one of the most exclusive

nightclubs in Vegas, that meant this party was a bit over-the-top, which was one reason Annalise found herself alone in the shadows. Not only were most of those in attendance Dominic's friends and colleagues, but Annalise wasn't exactly in the partying mood.

Although she wouldn't let her own troubles infringe on Meredith and Dominic's day of celebration. But it was difficult to shake the feeling that she should be back at Magnifique, trying to track down the assholes actively stealing from her.

"A woman as beautiful as you shouldn't be alone in the corner."

Annalise turned to stare at the tall, dark and handsome man standing in front of her. A tingle of awareness shot down her spine, unwanted and inconvenient.

Raising an eyebrow, she asked, "Is that a lame attempt at 'no one puts Baby in a corner'?"

"No, merely an observation." A twinkle of amusement flashed through the steel-gray eyes watching her.

He was teasing her, something she might have found charming on anyone else. But considering *who* was standing beside her… "You might find it more successful on someone who isn't intimately familiar with your ability to con and manipulate."

Surprise shot across the sharp features of his face before he managed to cover it up.

Oh, Annalise knew him. She remembered, vividly, the night her father had thrown Luca Kilpatrick out of Magnifique for cheating eight years ago.

That aristocratic face with the charming, steely eyes would be hard to forget. Not to mention the long, powerful body that didn't belong on a guy who spent hours sitting at a card table.

Back then, Annalise had been an intern, soaking up every piece of knowledge she could from her father. Including the less savory aspects of running a casino. Like dealing with cheaters.

But that was a long time ago.

With a shrug, Annalise dismissed him. "Why don't you run along before I make a visit to security? I'm sure my brother wouldn't appreciate you crashing his party."

A dark, knowing grin lit up Luca's face. Leaning close, the warmth of Luca's breath brushed across her exposed skin, sending goose bumps rushing down her chest, as he murmured, "Sweetheart, Dominic invited me. He thought it might be a good way to introduce you to the man you asked him to hire."

Crap. She hastily crossed her arms over her chest to hide her suddenly erect nipples. Wait. What had he just said?

Pulling back, Luca slipped his hands into his pockets and shrugged. "Looks like I'm your newly hired consultant. I hear you have a little cheating problem."

The delight in his eyes really pissed her off. Damn him, he was enjoying this.

"Nothing about this problem is little," including

the amount of money that had already been stolen from her family's business. "And there's not a snowball's chance in hell you're stepping foot inside Magnifique. You were blackballed, remember. Banished."

Luca shrugged, completely unconcerned. "Suit yourself."

Annalise was going to kill her brother.

* * * * *

Look for Annalise's story, coming soon!

And don't miss the Bad Billionaires trilogy from Kira Sinclair and Harlequin Desire:

The Rebel's Redemption
The Devil's Bargain
The Sinner's Secret

#2839 WHAT HE WANTS FOR CHRISTMAS
Westmoreland Legacy: The Outlaws • by Brenda Jackson
After a decade apart, COO Sloan Outlaw isn't looking to get back with ex Lesley Cassidy. But with her company facing a hostile takeover, he offers his assistance...if she joins him at his luxury cabin. But when they find themselves snowed in, the heat ignites...

#2840 HOW TO HANDLE A HEARTBREAKER
Texas Cattleman's Club: Fathers and Sons • by Joss Wood
Gaining independence from her wealthy family, officer and law student Hayley Lopez is rarely intimidated, especially by the likes of billionaire playboy developer Jackson Michaels. An advocate for the underdog, Hayley clashes often with Jackson. But will one hot night together change everything?

#2841 THE WRONG MR. RIGHT
Dynasties: The Carey Center • by Maureen Child
For contractor Hannah Yates, the offer to work on CEO Bennett Carey's project is a boon. Hired to repair his luxury namesake restaurant, she finds his constant presence and good looks...distracting. Burned before, she won't lose focus, but the sparks between them can't be ignored...

#2842 HOLIDAY PLAYBOOK
Locketts of Tuxedo Park • by Yahrah St. John
Advertising exec Giana Lockett has a lot to prove to her football dynasty family, and landing sports drink CEO Wynn Starks's account is crucial. But their undeniable attraction is an unforeseen complication. Will they be able to make the winning play to save their relationship and business deal?

#2843 INCONVENIENT ATTRACTION
The Eddington Heirs • by Zuri Day
When wealthy businessman Cayden Barker is blindsided by Avery Gray, it's not just by her beauty—her car accidently hits his. And then they meet again unexpectedly—at the country club where he's a member and she's employed. Is this off-limits match meant to last?

#2844 BACKSTAGE BENEFITS
Devereaux Inc. • by LaQuette
TV producer Josiah Manning needs to secure lifestyle guru Lyric Smith as host of his new show. As tempting as the offer—and producer—is, Lyric is hesitant. But as a rival emerges, will they take the stage together or let the curtain fall on their sizzling chemistry?

---

*After a decade apart, COO Sloan Outlaw
isn't looking to get back with ex Lesley Cassidy.
But with her company facing a hostile takeover,
he offers his assistance…if she joins him at his luxury
cabin. But when they find themselves snowed in,
the heat ignites…*

Read on for a sneak peek at
What He Wants for Christmas
by New York Times *bestselling author Brenda Jackson.*

"What do you want to ask me, Sloan?"

He drew in a deep breath. "I need to know what made you come looking for me last night."

She broke eye contact with him and glanced out the window, not saying anything for a moment. "You were gone longer than you said you would be. I got worried. It was either go see what was taking you so long or pace the floor with worry even more. I chose the former."

"But the weather had turned into a blizzard, Les." He then realized he'd called her what he'd normally called her while they'd been together. She had been Les and not Leslie.

"I know that. I also knew you were out there in it. I tried to convince myself that you could take care of yourself, but I also knew with the amount of wind blowing and snow coming down that anything could have happened."

She paused again before saying, "Chances are, you would have made it back to the cabin, but I couldn't risk the chance you would not have."

He tried not to concentrate on the sadness he heard in her voice and saw in her eyes. Instead, he concentrated on her mouth and in doing so was reminded of just how it tasted. "Not sure if I would have made it back, Les. My head was hurting, and it was getting harder and harder to make my body move because I was so cold. Hell, I wasn't even sure I was going in the right direction. I regret you put your own life at risk, but I'm damn glad you were there when I needed you."

"Just like you were there for me and my company when I needed you, Sloan," she said softly.

Her words made him realize that they'd been there for each other when it had mattered the most. He didn't want to think what would have been the outcome if he'd been at the cabin alone as originally planned and the snowstorm hit. Nor did he want to think what would have happened to her and her company if Redford hadn't told him what was going on. The potential outcome of either made him shiver.

"You're still cold. I'd better go and get that hot chocolate going," she said, shifting to get up and reach for her clothes.

"Don't go yet," he said, not ready for any distance to be put between them or their bodies.

She glanced over at him. Their gazes held and then, as if she'd just noticed his erection pressing against her thigh, she said, "You do know the only reason why we're naked in this sleeping bag together, right?"

He nodded. "Yes. Because I needed your body's heat last night." He inched his mouth closer to hers and then said, "Only problem is, I still need your body's heat, Les. But now I need it for a totally different reason."

And then he leaned in and kissed her.

Don't miss what happens next in...
What He Wants for Christmas *by Brenda Jackson,*
the next book in her Westmoreland Legacy:
The Outlaws series!

Available December 2021 wherever
Harlequin Desire books and ebooks are sold.

Harlequin.com